THE
FOREVER MAN
COLLECTION

Sam Graham

Alban Lake Publishing

The Forever Man Collection
Sam Graham

The Forever Man Collection is a work of fiction. Names, characters, places, and incidents are products of the author's imagination. Any resemblance to actual events or persons, living or dead, is entirely coincidental.

Story copyrights owned by Sam Graham
Cover illustration by Pete Linforth
Cover design by Karen Otto

First Printing
March 2020

Alban Lake Publishing
P.O. Box 141
Colo, Iowa 50056-0141 USA
e-mail: albanlake@yahoo.com

Visit www.albanlakepublishing.com for online science fiction, fantasy, horror, scifaiku, and more. Stop by our online bookstore at www.irbstore.co for novels, magazines, anthologies, and collections. Support the small, independent press and your First Amendment rights.

To Matt and Ash, for all the encouragement

FORWARD

A tempestuous storm of unnatural proportions which threatens the world. A terrifying armada of cannibals riding a convoy pulled by corpses, reanimated by parasitic grass. A town with walls comprised of the liquefied remains of those killed by 'The Return'. The stories contained within this book are packed to the brim with nightmarishly creative imagery; the sort of imagery which shows that there is far more to fantasy than just castles, wizards, and dragons.

I have known Sam for neigh on a decade now (gods, has it been that long?) and for me The Lord of the Last Day cycle is the perfect representation of Sam. Depicted in these three stories is a bleak, unique world, which could only have come from someone who has lived and breathed genre fiction for his entire life.

The stories deposit us into a savage post-apocalyptic world set some years after an event known simply as 'The Return'. Little information is provided on 'The Return' but we are invariably told that during this time, vast, impossibly ancient, cosmic monstrosities returned to Earth to reclaim it for themselves. What they left behind is a world functionally recognisable as our own (especially for those who hail from East Yorkshire, England), but forever changed. Society collapsed and was supplanted by ragtag townships and brutal tribes. The natural order was not merely destroyed, but wildly transformed so that the alien has become the new normal.

And at its heart, 'the new normal' is what The Lord of the Last Day is all about. Sam has designed a world that is not interested in mourning the dead order, but is learning to live what the world has become. For many—including our protagonist, the equally heroic and uncompromising wanderer, Corvin—the old world is simply a myth—known only to those unfortunate

few who lived through 'The Return'. Corvin under-
stands the rules of this brave new world, its
phenomena, its creatures, and its industries, because
he was born into it. And as we follow Corvin, little time
is spent on eulogising the fallen world—it does not
serve Corvin in his simple goal of surviving.

Divide The Lord of the Last Day into its base
influences and you'll find Michael Moorcock's seminal
sword and sorcery series about an albino antihero,
Elric of Melniboné; H.P. Lovecraft's legendary brand of
cosmic horror, which combines an indifference to humanity, an incomprehensible universe, and colossal
unknowable abominations; the sublime Roadside
Picnic by Arkady and Boris Strugatsky in which the
mundane is transformed into the preternatural by an
alien visit to Earth. And perhaps you'll also dig up a
little Mad Max: the post-apocalyptic film series about
a lone wanderer in a world reclaimed by violence and
insanity.

Sam combines these wildly different influences
with an understanding of how fantasy usually works.
The Lord of the Last Day plays with the expectation
these fantasy tropes create. Take the first story, for
example. At the very core is a tale in which the hero is
taken to a strange fiefdom, mistreated by its cruel
ruler, and liberates the maiden. Once you have read
the story, however, you will understand how this
fantasy tale makes the familiar very, very different. As
'The Return' did to his fictional world, Sam has taken
the fantasy story, turned it inside out, and made it his
own.

Ashley Bailey

TABLE OF CONTENTS

Sam Graham

THE LORD OF THE LAST DAY

The Lord of the Last Day

CORVIN

The deadgrass field where the soldiers found Corvin was once a nature reserve that had thrived with trees and streams and animal life. But things were no longer as they once were.

Corvin waited for them to come. There was no use trying to hide from them; the field was a square mile of flat land with no cover to conceal him. Nothing but the deadgrass and him in the middle. They had seen him already. Their voices carried on the wind. All three of them were asking what kind of death wish he must have to be sitting alone in the middle of all that deadgrass.

Corvin sighed as he asked himself the same question. The sweet, ensnaring fragrance of the deadgrass was strongest here close to the river. He had sat there for hours watching the pale red sky go by, and each passing moment took an act of will to resist the deadgrass' allure. It wanted him to eat it. Corvin knew the danger, so why had he chosen to make camp here on this particular spot? The answer was obvious to him, though he was loathed to admit it.

In that moment a strange despair awoke inside him. A voice that wasn't his own whispered directly into his mind, softly hinting that the deadgrass was the best thing for him; the only thing left for him. After all, the Lesser One's trail had gone cold months ago. There was no way he'd be able to hunt the creature now. He had failed as a protector; now he had failed as an avenger. After everything he had lost, there was no sense in carrying on.

His hand moved unconsciously to the reeds of deadgrass beside him. The bristles felt coarse between his fingers. The tender voice urged him to pick them as the scent around him flared, smothering him as he pulled the yellow strands from the soil. It was only when he heard the soldiers close behind him that looked down at the deadgrass in his hand and realised what he was about to do. In that moment he snapped out of the trance. The voice was silenced and the scent dissipated as he regained control. Corvin scolded himself for letting his will falter, for allowing the dead-grass manipulate his thoughts and lure him in like that. How long had it been subtlety working on him? Was it the reason he'd made camp here? As he'd passed the field earlier that day, had it planted the idea then? His will restored, he dropped the reeds before the soldiers had chance to see.

The oldest of the soldiers approached while the other two kept back. Corvin assumed he was the leader, because he was considerably older than the others and was the only one carrying a shotgun. Corvin made a mental note of their positions around him as he braced for an attack from his flank, but to his surprise, the leader asked him to come with them.

"Is that a real request, or are you planning to make that decision for me?" Corvin pulled his black cloak around his shoulders. From beneath his wide-brimmed hat the soldiers saw a thick scar running across the ridge of a hooked nose. His narrow eyes passed between them, taking each of them in. The other two looked elsewhere when Corvin's gaze met theirs, but the leader wasn't put off at all. He held the man in black's gaze in earnest and returned it with the same potency and curiosity, making the same deductions about Corvin that he made about them. The other two were inexperienced and weak, but that one... That one had seen more than most.

That one was dangerous.

"You tell me. Make your decision while it's still yours to make." Captain Bailey stepped closer, trampling the shimmering yellow deadgrass beside the fire. The youngest of his troops moved a hand to his sword while the larger one drew a handgun from the back of his trousers. Bailey raised the barrel of his Remington cautiously. His hands tensed. "You don't have long."

Corvin looked at the strands of deadgrass he'd pulled on the ground as he deliberated the quickest way to end the confrontation. He reckoned he could get past from the three of them; slip through as they fumbled with their weapons and flee. But those guns... Provided they'd actually found some ammunition for them and weren't just for show, they were a problem. A risk. He couldn't afford risks like that.

But even if he did manage to escape, there was only the river to run to. He stared at the mile-wide span of blackened ooze the elders had called the Humber. To the West, a suspension bridge had collapsed into it some undeterminable time ago; the broken chunks of road and concrete struts had formed a dam. About a mile in the other direction, an enormous blue and white ferry laid capsized in its dock. The surfaced part of the ship was overgrown with a sinewy black mass that stretched up from the river itself. That same mass was encroaching the land too, creeping up and gaining a foothold on the soil a few hundred yards away from him. From this distance Corvin couldn't tell if it was some kind of animal, or vegetation and he didn't care to find out. Something was in there, he knew that much.

Running was no option at all.

Besides, the deadgrass had been right. The things it had whispered to him were all true. He had lost his quarry. He had hunted it for months, following the trail of missing children and nightmares. The exact point at which he'd lost it, he couldn't say, but three months was more than enough time for the Lesser One to escape him. To change. To reintegrate itself with a population to destroy them from within the same way it had done his. Only with Corvin it had done more than that. So much more.

Corvin had chosen this spot in the deadgrass field, because he had given up. The promise he'd made was broken. These soldiers had found him a failure. But even though the deadgrass spoke the truth, he was not prepared to die here, now, in this field.

The soldiers were growing impatient.

Corvin kicked a heap of dirt on to the campfire and stood up. The soldiers jumped back and drew their weapons, but the man in black simply stretched his arms. Undisguised by his cloak, the guards saw he stood taller than them. He was lanky, with lean arms and legs and a gaunt, hungered face. Thin metal plates were stitched over the shoulders and forearms of his shirt. Maybe once they had been shiny and new, but now they were scratched and dented.

"I think I'll walk with you fellows for a while then." The man in black said.

"Good choice." Bailey said, keeping his gun ready.

They searched him for weapons, only to find that he carried none, and no supplies, or tools either, then they handcuffed his wrists together in front of him. He didn't try to stop them. As well as a blade each, Corvin saw that each soldier wore a metal plate over his chest and back that looked like pieces cut from a car bonnet, tied together with rope and slung over their shoulders. Hard plastic pads protected their elbows and knees and their swords were crude hunks of sharpened metal, hammered and twisted into shape and still bearing the marks of their inept creation. Though their armour was unmarked, they all wore the same teal shirt underneath, which Corvin assumed signified them as being from somewhere specific. The only things that set Captain Bailey apart from his men were his gun, his greying beard and that foreboding look in his eyes as he studied his prisoner.

They cut across the deadgrass fields and followed the blackened river for half a day, then turned south, making a point to avoid the crumbling roads. By dusk they approached the remains of a town that, according to Captain Bailey, elders used to call Scunthorpe. The youngest soldier protested when Bailey indicated they were to make camp within its ruins, but a glance silenced him. None of them, not even Bailey liked the idea, but the old man knew it was the safest place from any wandering crossbreeds or scavengers.

As they stepped within the town limits the wind ended with a sigh and then there was nothing. The absence was immediately noticeable as a gloom that permeated the streets and dampened the spirit. Cars lined the roads, still since the moment the skies had ripped open, their bodywork rusted and their tyres rotted away. Some of their skeletal drivers still faced upwards at the sky, but most had collapsed into a pile.

As they proceeded into Scunthorpe, each of them became aware of the noises they made. Every footstep was muted, like the air here was thicker and thus harder for noise to penetrate. Even their breathing felt distant. Though they moved as normal, they felt as though they were underwater. They all yearned for some sign of civilization. Something to assure them they hadn't succumbed to this otherworldly vacuum, but there was no sign of life. The ruins were vacant. Decades of abandonment and the ravaging effects of The Return had left the city a hulking ossuary, held up precariously by its bones, waiting for them to turn to dust so the town could finally collapse and disappear.

The solitude was absolute. They felt it more than ever.

But even so, Bailey knew they would be safe until morning. Places of great mourning like these retained a kind of lingering energy that some crossbreeds could sense, so they stayed away to spare their own sanity. He thought it ironic that even they, the bastard children of The Return, couldn't cope with the barrage of voices screaming through their minds, reliving their deaths over and over.

As the black-scarred sun descended, the soldiers built a small fire in the town square. Corvin's handcuffs were adjusted and he was fastened to a crooked lamppost with his hands behind his back. His legs ached from the marching, but he looked over at Bailey and saw he was worse. Tiredness was written all over his body. The old man planted the butt of his shotgun in the pavement and leaned against it, a slight wheeze in every breath.

They sat in silence for a while, each man avoiding the hollow town in the dark, afraid to acknowledge that they were afraid. Corvin broke the silence and asked where he was being taken and why.

Bailey didn't look up from the ground. "It's up to the Lord to decide where you'll be put to work. We need people for the mines. Maybe the farms, don't know."

The youngest of the group shuffled over, staying within the hue of the firelight. He was the youngest by a long way. Corvin put him at fifteen at best. Scrawny. Pathetic facial hair covered his top lip. Hadn't yet had the growth spurt that would develop him into a man. "Just pray you don't get put in the breeding pit. There's noises come from there you wouldn't believe."

Bailey sighed. "Shut up, Farama. You'll scare him half to death before we even get there."

"I'm only trying to help him. And maybe he ought to be scared. Death's a mercy compared to that. It's not natural what goes on in there. I've seen it with my own eyes, I have."

"We've all seen it." Bailey said ruefully.

"Yeah, and I bet you wanted a go, didn't you?" The other soldier, the largest one of the three said with a snigger, "finally get your cherry popped, eh lad?"

"Yeah right. You think I'd want a go with that thing? Only you think you're funny, Duncan." Farama spat back, but Corvin could tell he was more hurt than he let show.

"I wouldn't mind a go, all things considered. Reckon it'd be alright until, you know." Duncan grinned.

"Well go on then. And leave me alone, I've told you before. And so's the Captain." Farama looked to Bailey for support, but the old man didn't give it.

Duncan wrapped his surly arm around Farama's shoulder and shook him. "Don't worry about him, prisoner. He's just upset because no woman'll see to him. And it's not for lack of trying either, believe you me." He laughed.

Farama shoved the arm off and shuffled closer to the Captain.

"Just shut the hell up, the pair of you. I'm sick of it." Bailey snapped, but his voice, even though raised, did not carry far. "Give me a moment's peace. Besides, even if he does get sent there, Lord Auster won't want him limp-dicked with fright, will he?" Bailey cast them both a glance to silence them, but in his heart, he agreed with the kid. Corvin could see it in his eyes.

"Oh, he won't be." The big soldier muttered, staring at the prisoner. "It'll see to that."

Farama turned to Corvin. "What were you doing in the deadgrass fields anyway? Don't you know they're dangerous?"

"Don't expect much out of him, kid." Duncan said between biting his fingernails and spitting them into the fire. "Looks like he's gone already. No man sits in those fields for that long and doesn't eat some of it. Reckon we'll wake up tomorrow and he'll be covered in the stuff. It's probably growing inside him now. It'll be growing out of his skin by breakfast."

"Ignore him." Farama whispered to Corvin. "But seriously, where are you from? What's your name?"

Corvin leaned in towards Farama. He looked him in the eye now that they were side by side and the young soldier looked down at his boots. "You said pray

I'm not sent to that breeding pit?" The kid nodded. "Pray to what, exactly?"

The sun had disappeared. The pale red sky had become a sheet of black without clouds, or stars. The space above them was a stark barren void. As empty as the town.

The soldiers turned in for the night with Duncan taking first watch. He kept his eye on Corvin and his gun in his hand the entire time.

As Corvin looked up at the nothingful sky, he quietly sized up his options. The name Bailey dropped told him all he needed to know about the danger he was in. He'd heard of this 'Lord Auster' a few times since setting out to hunt the Lesser One, but only once by that name. In the months since losing his quarry, he must have wandered off course further than he'd realised. In the outlying settlements, Lord Auster was known as the Crossbreed King, and people had a tendency not to live long in his service. Now Corvin had wound up his prisoner.

I should have killed them in the field, he thought.

THE CROSSBREED KING

The walls around the keep were a mismatched structure of junked cars heaped fifteen feet high. Corvin and the soldiers saw it in the distance as the black-scarred sun reached its peak in the clear red sky. They had all been eager to leave Scunthorpe as soon as possible, so they left before dawn. It had been a long morning of walking up a steady slope, and though Corvin had not slept at all that night, the toll of their journey showed on Captain Bailey the most. The old man limped, stooping slightly as they crested the hill, pushing his weathered hands down on his knees for strength.

Bailey gave a long sigh of relief as the barricade of vehicles came over the horizon. He was home. Soon he could rest and massage his aches. But instead of stopping to catch his breath and savour the moment, Bailey shoved Corvin through the gates and marched him straight to the keep. With his finger on the shotgun's trigger, he asked his prisoner to kneel on the broken concrete overgrowing with weeds.

"Another of your pretend requests?" Corvin smirked. Bailey's brow creased, but he didn't say anything. The old man was still panting. His cheeks flushed red beneath his greying facial hair. Corvin tutted and complied. They waited for the Crossbreed King.

The keep itself was once a Protestant church; the centre-point of a village that had been reduced to rubble. Although the church was the only building that had survived The Return intact, its outer walls were blasted with the melted down flesh and bones of the area's former residents. Bodies of hundreds of men and women, possibly more, were fused together into one large mass. Hands and parts of faces could be

11

made out, but all had since dried up decades ago and set over the brickwork of the church like plaster. Even though he had lived alongside it for years, Bailey still grimaced when he saw it.

Villagers and more soldiers shambled out from their tents and sheet-metal homes and gathered around, anxious to see the spectacle about to unfold. Corvin counted only fifteen soldiers and around twice that in villagers. Humans by the look of them; thin, pale, malnourished skin, drab, dirt-stained hung off them, but all purebreeds. He didn't understand. How could they live under the rule of a Crossbreed? In all the places he'd been, he'd never known it.

But there was something else about them Corvin couldn't put his finger on. Something not right. It wasn't until he saw it on the chapped skin of a little girl that it became as clear as the black mark that streaked across the sun. Three thin red lines ran from her ear down to her collarbone. Fingernails scratches. They stood out against her dry skin and it was the same on every one of them. Even on the soldiers who apprehended him. Now, in the full light of day, he saw the marks on Bailey and Duncan too. Corvin sighed. He understood what it meant.

It meant that by getting lost, he'd found his quarry. The Lesser One he hunted had been here recently; maybe still was. The weeks of directionless searching had not been wasted.

It meant that now he had a task to perform. One he wasn't looking forward to.

But his bloody deed would have to come later. Just then, the double-doors of the keep creaked as they parted. Flakes of dried flesh fell like silt from the walls, and the soldiers and the villagers bowed their heads as the Crossbreed King emerged.

Again Corvin was confused. This man they called the Crossbreed King was human. Not a crossbreed at all, but pure, with none of the dilution from the Lesser

Ones. So why did people call him that? What was going on?

"Who is this man, Captain Bailey?" Lord Auster nodded unremarkably towards Corvin. The rolls of skin underneath his chin trembled as he spoke. Around his forehead was a metal band marked with symbols Corvin couldn't read, but presumed they were some mark of his position. The dark blue jacket he wore did little to cover his stomach, but the tassels on the shoulders and the coloured ribbons on the left side marked him as above the rest, drawing the eye to him as the only colour in a village of grey and brown.

"Found him in the deadgrass fields out by the river, sir." Captain Bailey stepped forward, head held high.

"So why bring him to me if he's been eating dead-grass? Just chuck him away and let nature take its course."

"He wasn't eating any of the deadgrass, sir."

Now Auster eyed Corvin with interest. "Really? Wasn't eating it? Are you sure he wasn't eating it before you found him?"

"If that was the case, my lord, he'd still be out there now. It'd already be growing out of him. We found him yesterday."

"Hmm, seems like a smart man." He stroked his chin and he leaned towards the man in black. "Are you a smart man, prisoner?"

"Depends on what you're asking me." This close up, Corvin could see the same red marks on the Cross-breed King's wide neck, but it was more than just marks with him. His skin was turning a sickly grey, already flaking off in clumps at the sides of his neck and hairline. It was only slight, so minute that his followers wouldn't have noticed yet, but Corvin knew what to look for. He'd seen it before. It was what started his hunt in the first place.

The conversation was quiet. Just the two of them now. "What were you doing out in the deadgrass if you weren't trying to eat it? I'm curious, how did you manage to resist? I've seen the most iron-willed give in to its scent."

Corvin thought back to that voice whispering in his mind, urging him to become one with the deadgrass. How it fed off his despair. His blood went cold, but he did not allow it to show to the Crossbreed King. "And what happened to these people of such great will?" Corvin said, not returning the gaze.

"Oh I think you already know that."

"Maybe." Now Corvin looked up at him. "And if I did, it'd be that thought that kept me from eating that stuff no matter how hard it tried to get me."

Auster straightened up, not amused and somewhat put out by Corvin's lack of respect. He pondered over the man's wide-brimmed black hat, his black cloak, the crude metal plating over the shoulders and forearms of his black shirt, all of which looked self-made and would offer no protection from the harshness of the world. "What's your name, prisoner?" Auster lifted his hat and looked into the man's sallow eyes. He didn't find any of the reverence that everyone else in the square gave him. He didn't find anything at all. They just looked forward, through him, like he wasn't there.

"Corvin."

"Is that your full name?"

"Do I need a longer one?"

Lord Auster laughed. It was a name he had never come across before, but he thought nothing of it. Besides, a name was just what someone answered to, as far as he was concerned. Auster raised his arms out and gestured to their surroundings "Well, I am the lord of this town. That makes me Lord Auster."

Corvin didn't look impressed. "Does it?"

"It does. My father, Lord Auster Senior created it."

Corvin looked around at the domes of sheet metal held together by old, fraying bits of rope. Between the houses were the muddy pathways here Auster's cursed disciples stood up to their ankles in filth. "All by himself eh? Impressive."

Auster struck the man across the cheek. "For a man blinded by The Return, it is actually." He composed himself. "He was a tradesman. His instruction built this place. They proclaimed him Lord before he was killed by a Fear Eater. What would you, without a title, know about it?"

Corvin sighed. There was never any point in reasoning with Auster. "Apparently nothing."

The fat man nodded triumphantly. "You have no title. You are no one."

Auster turned on his heel and shuffled back towards the keep doors. He beckoned Captain Bailey over and it didn't take them long to discuss the prisoner's fate.

"You're off to the breeding pit, pal. Sorry." Captain Bailey said, ordering Farama and Duncan to get him on his feet. Duncan sniggered as they stood Corvin up. As they turned to leave, the man in black called out.

"Roses in a field of broken glass." Everyone: the soldiers, the villagers, even Auster himself stopped dead. Whispers passed between the villagers. Corvin felt the grip on his arms loosen and the Crossbreed King looked at him in terror. "Roses. You've dreamt about them, haven't you? You don't know what a rose is, but you've had the dreams. You've all have had the dreams. Roses, they look like void stalks, surrounded by shards of broken glass like those in the keep windows. Tell me you've had them. You too, Auster. You've been having them the longest. Tell me I'm wrong."

Lord Auster was shaking. His eyes darted between his subjects as the mutters from the villagers increased. Just who was this stranger and how did he know about the nightmares? Auster felt a fear he couldn't name. His subjects were questioning it too.

And his troops. The whispers were becoming aggravated mutters and angry glares. Why were they staring at him? This stranger had caused this. If he left it unchecked, it could lead to dissent. He could feel his control slipping. He began to pant. A Lord was only a Lord so long as he could maintain his kingdom. This stranger had to go—no, better yet; he had to be made an example of. "Captain, take him to the pit immediately. When he's finished, bring him back here and tie what's left of him to a post in the middle of the square."

The Crossbreed King hurried inside his keep.

THE BREEDING PIT

About a mile from the keep stood a tower. Corvin had seen on the horizon as he approached the keep that morning and now, marching towards it, he kept his chin up and back straight to prevent the soldiers from sensing his apprehension. It loomed over him, tall and imposing; the fractured sun hung right above it, its shadow stretched over the surrounding dead-grass fields like a sinister finger. In those fields they had passed the remains of harvesters and tractors, one with a flatbed still hooked behind it. Their great tyres sagged; the petrol in their tanks had evaporated and leaked out as the seals had perished decades ago.

The original use of both the vehicles and the tower were lost to Auster's soldiers and the former protector, like so much knowledge before The Return. Elders had on several occasions tried to teach Corvin about something they called 'electricity'. He understood it to be a force that gave the dead metal life in the time before the gates had opened in space and the Earth was ravaged by their presence. But each time the sightless elders tried to explain, they would stop mid-sentence and be struck by a daze. Their minds fogged in confusion as though the knowledge had been erased.

But in their sightlessness, they had not seen what their world had become. Perhaps it was for the best. They'd all seen too much horror. That was why they'd ripped their own eyes out.

That hulking metal cylinder that loomed over Corvin, once a grain silo, was now Lord Auster's breeding pit.

Farama sighed as they neared the structure. "I'm sorry, friend. I know that doesn't help, but if there's anything I can say that might comfort you, it seems to be only momentary, then you'll forget the pain."

"If you're really that sorry then take these cuffs off and give me your weapon." Corvin said. Accepting sentimentality from the person dragging him to his doom was asking too much.

Duncan shoved Corvin forward with his handgun. "You'd like us to kill you now, wouldn't you? Spare you the pain?" Because of his sheer size, the armour over Duncan's chest was made from two separate plates of metal, bolted and hammered together with rivets. Veins bulged in his tanned arms and his hands looked strong enough to crush Corvin's skull. Like all the rest though, he wasn't immune. Those same marks were on his neck. "Oh, and you won't forget the pain, exactly. You'll have the memory of it sucked out of you." He laughed. When Corvin didn't say anything, Duncan snatched his hat and put it on himself. It didn't fit properly. "What you wear this thing for anyways? So, the birds can't see how ugly you are before it's too late? You should borrow it for a night, Farama. Might do you wonders if they don't know it's you." He laughed again. Corvin looked at the younger guard who had the same wounded expression as the night before.

Farama sighed. "I can't let you go. Captain Bailey's orders."

"He's back at the keep now. Besides, you always do everything you're told?" Corvin said.

"I have to be able to do things like this."

"Like what?" Corvin asked,

"Things that... I don't want to do."

"Really?"

The kid nodded. "If I want to be Captain one day. Captain Bailey doesn't always agree with his orders, but he told me when I first joined a few moons ago that being a leader means sometimes doing things that you don't agree with. I asked him how he does them and he said he's only following someone else's orders. They don't go against his own principles if the orders aren't given by him. Or something like that anyways. I don't remember all of it. It was quite confusing."

"So, you're telling me that you'll get over murdering me, because since you didn't order me to this pit, it's not your problem, right?"

Farama wanted to say yes and agree like he knew he should, but he didn't. He didn't say anything. Corvin laughed forlornly as he saw the dissonance on the kid's face. Duncan thought they were both talking a load of rubbish.

The guards on the door at the pit said someone was already in there, so Duncan and Farama took Corvin to a small wooden barn further along the field. There he was thrown into a cell with one other person and a dozen men in other cells. The prisoners were rowdy when the guards entered, reaching for them, shouting at them, hurling insults, but as the doors closed and the room went dark, the mood quickly turned sombre. Corvin sat down on the soil and thought of how to escape, ignoring his cellmate in the corner while he listened to the prisoners' sob. Whispered conversations sparked up and Corvin turned his ear to them. From what he overheard, he judged that the other men were due for the breeding pit too. And he was surprised to learn that his own cellmate, the one cowering in the corner, was a woman.

She shrank away as Corvin approached. A jute shroud wrapped around her save for her bare hands and feet. The failed protector raised his hands, still fastened together, palms open as a gesture of peace as he approached, then slowly knelt down next to her. She was trembling, flattened herself against the corner wall, whimpering.

"What are you doing here?" Corvin said, putting on as soft a voice as he could, but he still sounded cold.

"Please, not again." Her voice was barely above a squeak. She brought her knees up to her chin and wrapped her arms around her legs.

"Answer my question." Corvin touched the shroud over her face. She flinched away and tried to shake his hands off, but he grabbed the cloth and held it tight in a fist. "I won't ask a second time."

"I'm... I'm for the Lord."

"What do you mean?"

"A substitute for his Lady." The shroud slipped from her legs and in the dim light from a crack in the roof he could see the top of her thighs were covered in bruises. Her skin was soft and young.

"He did these to you?"

She bit her lip. Corvin tried to pinpoint how old she was. He put her around mid-teens. "Not all of them."

"Don't trust her." A voice came from a cell at the far side of the barn. Corvin turned to face the voice in the dark and in the same motion, pinned the girl to the wall by her throat with both hands in case she tried something while his back was turned. The girl yelped and fought to wrestle free, but the more she struggled, the tighter he squeezed.

"What do you mean?" Corvin said to the voice.

"She gave those to herself, those bruises. We can always hear her, writhing around in the dark, tending to herself until she's bruised and bloody. That's why the Crossbreed King keeps her locked up out here. Even he can't handle her. Just gets her brought to him when he fancies a go."

Corvin could feel the pulse in the girl's neck racing. Her skin was warm and unspoiled. His hands were rough.

"Save me." She choked. One of them was lying. Was she the liar, or the victim? Being locked up with a liar was being locked up with a threat. And Corvin had experienced too many surprise attacks during his training as protector to let his guard down even when he was alone. It'd be wise to snap her neck now, just in case, he told himself, ensure his safety in the cell, but then he'd lose any chance of escape once Auster found out. He pulled the jute cloth away from her and for a moment Corvin was taken aback. Wide eyes, as blue as the former world's sky, stared helplessly into his. Deep within them he saw she was terrified out of her mind. She was as beautiful as she was fragile. Cold. Naked. He traced his eyes from her freckled cheeks down to her throat and he sighed when he saw it.

Her neck was clean. No scratches. Nothing. She alone was, as of yet, untouched by the Lesser One's plague.

He released her and wrapped the shroud around her thin body. She coughed as she caught her breath and by that time, Corvin was leaning against the bars at the other side of the cell. She moved beside him and whispered: "Will you, please? That man, Auster, he hurts."

Corvin sighed. She was the only one he might be able to save. "Aye child. I'll try." He turned back to her. "What's your name?"

"Natalia."

Corvin slid down the bars and sat on the earthen floor. The girl sat down beside him and rested her head on his shoulder.

"How did you end up here?" Corvin whispered.

"Father sold me to the Crossbreed King. He said I was only good for one kind of work."

"And where is he now?"

"Auster had him sent to the breeding pit. Said it's easier than paying for me."

"And he keeps you out here?"

Natalia nodded. "He has me brought to his bed when he needs me, then sends me back here."

"Have you ever slept in the keep?"

"He doesn't let me." Natalia sobbed. Her tears soaked into Corvin's shirt.

"That will be why you're unaffected. Sleeping here puts you out of its reach. The beast must be hidden among the villagers in the keep somewhere."

The girl sat up. "What are you talking about?"

Corvin sighed. "Nothing, child. I'll explain another time."

The doors of the barn were kicked open, letting in a scream from the breeding pit that turned Corvin's blood cold. In walked Farama and Duncan, still wearing Corvin's hat. "Right, you're up, pal." Duncan said as Farama unlocked his cell. Natalia retreated.

"Still not your orders, eh kid?" Corvin said when Farama refused to look at him. Corvin nodded to Natalia as he was led away. The soldiers marched him across the field to the breeding pit.

A corpse was being dragged out of the entrance as they neared. Then Corvin saw that it wasn't a corpse. The body was withered and whatever went on in the pit had left the skin brittle and clinging to the bones. The eyeballs were bright red from the bursting of the blood vessels, but somehow the thing was still alive. It babbled, its teeth hanging loose in its dried gums and its gnarled fingers twisted like tree branches. Corvin thought the thing better resembled a dried-up tree now more than the human being it once was. Looking down the body, Corvin saw that the former man's groin was overgrown with meaty polyps that pulsated.

"Don't worry. We keep them alive. They seem to relive it over and over in their heads, so like I said, you won't die." Duncan said.

"Give over." Farama muttered. The big guard just laughed. Farama turned away.

"What do you do with them?" Corvin said.

"We just let them wander." Duncan said. "They're on their own after that. Deadgrass usual takes care of them before long. Course, the Lord's got a special order for you though, hasn't he? Try to have fun in there, won't you? You might as well."

The guards by the silo door dropped the body and

turned. "Give her a rest, Duncan. This one's been in since sun-up."

Duncan shrugged. "Wish we could all go for that long, Gaff. It's not like she gets tired. Besides, Auster's orders. This one's to go in immediately. I'm betting he's done before sunset, tops."

"Well," Gaff looked Corvin over "not much on him is there? Looks like he's got some stamina though. I say midnight."

Duncan and the guard shook on it. After Farama took the cuffs off, Duncan shoved Corvin through the doorway and Gaff locked the door behind him.

The air in the pit was hot and moist. The edges of the silo were solid darkness, but a dim light emanated from candles on metal stands in the centre. Smoke fogged the air, and Corvin waded through the mist with caution, expecting attack from any direction. Lord Auster kept some sort of abomination here, something that would warp and reduce him to that former man he'd seen a moment ago, but the place was deathly silent. The metal walls muted sounds from outside completely. There was just him, the sound of his breathing and the beast that waited for him.

As he neared the light, he picked up a faint aroma. He recognised the distinct scent: acidic with a signature sweetness. He'd known it before and though it was strange to find it here, it was not altogether unwholesome. Then, when he saw what was in the centre of the light, he didn't understand at all.

Shackles clamped around her ankles and wrists and she lay on her back, propped up on her elbows. Chains extended around the back of the bed, fastening her to it. The bed itself had once been expensive and comfortable, but now the sheets were torn and sweat stained it dark. Straight, black hair hung down over the woman's face and as Corvin stepped into the light, she arched her back in response, accentuating her breasts. Everything about her was striking, poised to stir the sweet emotions. She gasped as her knees parted, deliberately showing him her full nakedness. The scent in the air intensified and Corvin found himself overwhelmed by it. It was stifling, nauseating, intoxicating, and most of all, enticing. He felt himself being drawn in by it.

Corvin relaxed and stepped up to the foot of the bed, positioning himself near her legs. Her mouth formed words without a sound. Her eyes were covered by a worn bandage that wrapped around her head. Corvin figured it stopped her from seeing the state of the offerings Auster threw her way. Around her forehead was a metal headband marked with the same symbols as Lord Auster's. She must be Lady Auster, he thought as his hands worked automatically to remove the buckle on his trousers. When he was ready for her, she positioned her hips so that she was ready for him too.

The scent was overwhelming now and he couldn't take his eyes off her. She was all he could see, all he could think of. He had to have her now. He ran his hands up her legs, feeling her hot sweat at the top as he prepared himself. His eardrums pulsed with the overpowering intoxication. So strong and alluring, it wasn't natural.

Corvin paused, and in that split-second he realised that he was right: It wasn't natural. Nothing about this woman, or how quickly he'd given himself over to her was natural. A key turned in his mind and, in the epiphany, he regained some of his senses. It made sense now.

The Crossbreed King was no crossbreed. But his wife was.

She bore no outward abnormalities like most crossbreeds, and coupled with her looks and figure, Corvin understood how she could have easily won her way into Auster's court and into his bed. But he kept her chained up all the way out here for a reason. And he kept that girl in the cells for the same reason too.

It was then that Corvin realised where Lady Auster's deformity lied. That same area where she'd enticed so many men. Where he himself was about to go. She sucked men dry and left them as husks. She was a bastard child of The Return. A crossbreed between the Lesser Old Ones that stayed on Earth and the surviving remnants of mankind. Their deformities differed with every offspring. She'd made the most of hers, using her attributes to gain status, but now it seemed the eldritch half of her was out of control. She was insatiable; a lust to breed and absorb that could never be slaked. Did she steal the vitality from men she enticed too? She looked so much younger than Auster, only slightly younger than Corvin, full-bodied and well nourished, unlike Natalia and those thralls back at the keep. No marks, or scars, or any signs of struggle on her skin. Was her crossbreed nature how she retained her beauty? How old was she really?

Corvin pushed himself away from her, but the scent in the air threatened to pull him back. As he forced himself to rebuckle his trousers, the Lady Auster sat up. Her mouth crooked into a dejected grimace.

"Go on. It won't hurt you right away. You'll enjoy me."

How many people had fallen into this trap? They had cells full of men and the guards were so casual about the breeding pit that it must have become routine. Like with the deadgrass, resisting her took an act of will. Corvin stepped around the bed to the Lady's head. She faced him, unseeing, and crooked her lip upwards. Again he felt himself wanting. Just to run his hand along her body, feel her muscles play against his. No! He ordered himself to keep control. He forced the image of the Lesser One he hunted to his mind. Reminded himself why he hunted it, of who it had taken from him, the things it had tricked him into doing.

He grabbed the woman's hair and yanked her head back. She opened her mouth, expecting him to thrust his onto hers, coaxing him to. Corvin fought the urge to steal one last kiss from the Crossbreed Queen as he broke her neck.

A King has his Reign...

It took the two guards a while to notice there was no sounds coming from inside the pit. On any given day it would be a short wait until the screams began. The screams would then devolve into a stuttering choke as the man inside had his essence drained. Then it would last for hours. Finally, they'd hear a groan of ecstasy from Lord Auster's crossbreed wife, then they'd go in and fetch the remains. But this time there was nothing. As they opened the door to investigate, Gaff immediately fell with a broken piece of wooden bedpost thrust into his eye. Before his body hit the ground, Corvin pulled his sword from his belt and without breaking his gait, run it through the other guard's neck.

Duncan was leaning against the wall of the prison barn, pondering whether to stretch his new hat to fit himself, or to give it to the kid, when he saw the attack. As the second guard fell, Duncan was already running across the field. His teal shirt dragged in the wind and his extra-large armour was heavy. He pulled his old Glock 17 from his belt and fired two shots at Corvin, but they missed as the man in black took cover behind the breeding pit door.

Duncan was still a good distance away, so Corvin decided he would wait for him to reload before closing that distance. It was unlikely that Duncan had salvaged enough bullets for a full magazine; he was surprised it even worked at all, but Duncan wasn't wasting bullets taking any more random potshots. For all his bravado, he was smarter than he came across. Corvin realised he would have to force the man's hand.

On the ground beside him, Gaff wasn't quite dead, so Corvin hauled him up and shoved him into the open field. A second later, three bullets ripped through him as Duncan emptied his clip into the first movement he saw. The firing stopped as Duncan's friend fell into the mud. Then Corvin sprinted across the deadgrass field.

His black clothing was light; the armour on his shoulders and forearms wasn't heavy. They didn't slow him down. The only thing that did was the sword.

Duncan thumbed his last two cartridges from his pocket into the empty magazine as his target rushed towards him. His hands shook with adrenaline, slowing the operation. The prisoner was more than half way across the field now.

Panicked, Duncan shoved the magazine into the port and cocked back the slide as Corvin raised the blade. The soldier managed a swift shot and a bolt of hot lead sunk into Corvin's shoulder, punching through his armour and staggering him back. But his sword arm had already swung. Had the gunshot missed, the swing would have been a killing blow. Had the sword been lighter, Duncan would not have had the chance. The end of the blade scraped down the soldier's face, over his eye and down to his chin, but it didn't cut deep enough.

Duncan clutched at his face as blood gushed from the wound. He raised his gun for another shot. Seeing this, the man in black dropped his sword and leapt. With both legs thrust forward, he kicked Duncan square in the chest. The soldier's last bullet went wide as both men fell to the ground. Duncan swore at the man in black. He rose to one knee and went to shoot again, but when the gun clicked empty, he threw it to the ground and drew his sword.

Corvin picked up his blade as he stood up, his shoulder in agony, and steadied himself. The sword was crude; a sharpened hunk of metal, probably the remains of a metal fence before The Return, hammered flat and sharpened at the edges, then fitted with a crossguard. The huge soldier kept one blood-soaked hand over his face as he advanced, holding his sword with the other.

His opening swing was powerful, pulled back and swung in a wide arc, but clumsy and telegraphed, fueled by frenzy. Corvin parried it easily, then another from the opposite direction. Corvin retreated as he parried two more attacks, deflected a lunge to one side, then sidestepped an overhead chop from Duncan. The soldier let out a frustrated cry as he used both hands to put all his weight behind his next attack, aiming to batter through the protector's defence and cleave him in half. There was a deafening clang as the top end of Duncan's blade was met near Corvin's hilt. The two pieces of metal bit into each other and locked together.

Still partially blinded, saliva dripping from his mouth and enraged by his prisoner's continued living, Duncan pushed against his opponent's blade, aiming to leave Corvin open for a finishing blow. The prisoner would die now, Duncan was sure of it. He would die bloody.

Corvin knew he could not match his opponent's strength, even with both hands. So, winding his hip, Corvin brought his sword up, keeping the hilt of his blade on the tip of Duncan's as he angled his blade downwards. The leverage allowed him control over Duncan's sword and in the same movement, pushed his attack away as he thrust the point of his sword into the soldier's chest, over his armour and just beneath his clavicle. Duncan's rage kept him from feeling the pain. It wasn't until Corvin twisted the blade that Duncan realised he was in the process of being killed. After which he fell to the ground, muttering to himself as he bled out.

Corvin took his hat back.

Farama trembled as he watched the battle from the barn. He was urinating round the back when he'd heard the gunfire. He rushed back and watched, secretly hoping Duncan would take care of the prisoner, so he wouldn't have to risk his own life. Now he cursed himself for following the orders that had led to this moment. His sword hung loose in his hands as Corvin approached. The man in black showed no sign of caution towards him. No attempt to be on guard as he stood directly in front of him. Farama tossed his weapon away.

"I'm... I'm sorry. So sorry, friend." He said, wiping away the tears.

"I'm not." Corvin thrust the blade through Farama's gut. The end of the sword protruded from his back and Farama was dead before his body hit the ground. Like Duncan, the deadgrass would be growing over his flesh before the day was over.

The barn full of prisoners was unguarded now. The remaining soldiers that were stationed there fled to the keep to alert the Crossbreed King. The prisoners cheered for Corvin as he approached Natalia's cell and knelt by the bars.

"Wait for me, child. I'll be back. Though it may not be until the morning." The girl nodded.

"You're making a terrible mistake." Said one of the prisoners, the same voice as before.

The girl took Corvin's hand through the bars and pressed it to her cheek. His skin was flecked with Farama's blood, but he felt warmth in Natalia's touch. As he stroked her face, the pain in his shoulder disappeared. Though he noticed this, he did not say anything.

"You're making a god damn mistake!" A prisoner said.

"I'll be back to release all of you." Corvin said. "Just wait for me."

Corvin left the cells and made for the keep of the Crossbreed King. He hated himself for lying to the prisoners, but he hoped that, if they knew what awaited them otherwise, they'd forgive him.

He took no pleasure in the killing. No sense of satisfaction and no desire for revenge drove him as he made his onslaught on Auster's keep.

A group of guards met him on the fields of yellow deadgrass between the breeding pit and the keep. Beneath the clear red sky, Corvin engaged them. Their number was few and he managed to keep them from rushing him all at once with Duncan's gun. While it was empty and while it was very possible there were no more bullets left in existence, the soldiers did not know that. All they saw was a gun, so they kept back, themselves only armed with swords and spears made from crooked branches that his own heavy sword easily smashed through.

As the last soldier fell, Corvin pulled the trigger, allowing him to hear it click and realise they had all been duped.

Panic erupted in the village as the former pro-tector's silhouette approached on the horizon. They ran screaming, barricading themselves in their flimsy homes and banging on the doors of the flesh-blasted church, begging to be let in. But the doors stayed firmly shut under Auster's orders. The troops on the inside wept as they listened to their friends and families being slaughtered by the man in black. A handful of villagers managed to flee before Corvin had reached them. They ran for the crumbling roads and the deadgrass fields. Corvin didn't chase them. In a way he felt sorry for them. The marks on their necks would make their fate much worse and much more prolonged than the ones who died today.

Captain Bailey stood listening by the keep doors until the sounds of violence outside had stopped. His skin was lacquered with sweat and the shotgun in his hands had become too heavy to hold. His men looked to him for orders, for hope, but he had nothing left. What had he wrought on them by bringing this person back to the keep? He'd seen it in the man's eyes when they first found him. Something strange. Something threatening. He'd thought the man could be put to good use in the mine, or the farm, but- Now this... He should have left him alone, or killed him right then.

Farama had been right. He should have trusted the boy. He had honest instincts, but instead he'd chosen to put his faith in his position. Captain of Auster's army. Giver of orders, answerable only to the Lord himself. Now what was he going to do? And where the hell was Auster? The men were looking at him, expecting him to get them out of this. The damn fools didn't know death when it came for them. He'd done it. He'd brought death to them all.

He hoped that Farama had managed to get away.

Three heavy knocks came from the double-doors. Bailey touched the scratch marks on his neck and gooseflesh ran down his spine. Roses in a field of broken glass. How did the stranger know?

"Get back." He ordered his men. They cleared away from the door as Bailey levelled his Remington. Only one shot, he thought. Miss and we're done.

And miss he did. A moment after knocking, one of the stained-glass windows behind him burst inwards. The Captain of Auster's army spun around and fired his only shot at the shape that rushed through. Though he missed, the intruder slumped to the floor, dead, his throat already cut in Corvin's slaughter.

Then Corvin climbed through the broken window, dropped down and took cover behind the pews. The guards under Bailey's command decided they valued their lives more than his orders as they unbarred the double-doors and fled together. Bailey cursed them under his breath as he watched them run, then turned back to see the man in black, his own prisoner, standing meters away from him. His black clothes and purloined sword were stained with blood.

"Quick or slow?" Corvin said. He stroked his long jaw.

"It was just orders. We were sent to round people up for work." Bailey dropped the empty shotgun. Another relic made useless. Corvin's dark eyes narrowed.

"Make your decision while it's still yours to make. You don't have long." Corvin said. "Quick or slow?" Captain Bailey looked back at the doorway. He calculated his odds. They didn't look great.

The Captain sighed. He knew when he was beaten. He'd lived a long, fraught life; Staved off death many times in his fifty-two years. Life had been hard, but in Auster's service he'd experienced some relative peace. He hoped that whatever came next was free from the Old Ones and the Lesser Ones and the Crossbreeds, deadgrass and shrieking mists and the Full-Moon Scourge... The shotgun on the floor was the same one he'd used to kill the Fear Eater that had killed Auster's father. Weeks of hunting on his own, awake all night, sleeping in the rain, tracking the thing to its cave. The ambush. The cold fear. The true version of events that he dare not tell anyone. He longed to be rid of memories like that.

Bailey's shoulders relaxed. He was ready. He closed his eyes, and as he exhaled one final time he whispered: "quick" and no sooner had the words left his mouth, his throat was cut.

The only word to come out of Lord Auster's mouth was "why?" over and over as he scrambled on his hands and knees, backing into the corner of his private quarters on the altar. To Auster, Corvin was an immense black shadow looming tall and menacing over him, stinking of blood and fury, carrying death in his hand.

"You shouldn't have done that to her." Corvin grit his teeth.

"I didn't know she was a crossbreed, alright." Auster quivered. "She, she abstained for years.

Wouldn't let me anywhere near her. Then she just went mad. Rampant even! She became insatiable, lusting after men, luring them in. She wouldn't stop. Killed people left right and centre. Then I learned about her deformity. I had to lock her up! It was for all our sakes! But I couldn't have her killed. I loved her all the same. I've loved her for years. What the hell would you know about it?" He sobbed.

"I'm not talking about your wife, you idiot."

"You can't do this to me. This is my keep. I earned it. They'd have all gone mad on deadgrass if it wasn't for me. Who are you to come for me? You're no one. Just some drifter. You're not a lord. You're just-" Auster put his hands over his face to protect himself as the man in black raised the blade.

"There are no lords anymore." Corvin thrust his sword, and Emelius Auster never got to learn who Corvin was talking about, or why it was a mercy for him and his people to die this way.

ONE LAST LORD

The smell of blood permeated on the wind that blew from the keep to the breeding pit. The majority of the prisoners were asleep as the sun rose, but they quickly roused when Corvin returned. The scent clung to his clothes.

"Come one. Quickly, free us, man." A prisoner said in the darkness.

"I will." Corvin said with a forlorn scowl. At first they thought the metallic scraping was the jangle of keys for the cell doors, but they quickly recognised it as a sword being unsheathed. "Forgive me. It's better this way."

There was little the prisoners could do to stop him. Soon their blood was in the air too. The stink of it would hang in the area for weeks until the rain washed it away.

At last they were alone. Corvin unlocked Natalia's cell. The young girl rushed him and he staggered back as she wrapped her arms around him, her lips seeking his cheeks and mouth, her small hands running through his hair.

Now, in the silence of the barn, only the girl's sobs and her hands pressing against him, Corvin realised just how exhausted he was. Every muscle was strained from battle. His shoulder was stiff, but pain-free since Natalia had touched him the night before. His eyes burned from lack of sleep. The adrenaline was dissipating and he felt himself slipping. Sleep was encroaching fast. Not yet! He forced himself to focus. I can't rest yet. Still things to do.

Pale red light poured in through the open door. The girl took a step back into it and let her shroud fall. Standing naked in the dawn light, Corvin could see that her hair was ginger and wavy, her skin was light and still free from the red scratches, and he could see the extent of the bruises that covered the tops of her legs.

Corvin picked her cloth up and wrapped it round her. "No, child. You come with me now. We'll find somewhere safe for you."

"But I want to be with you." She shrugged at the cloth. "I want—"

"We have to leave here. There might be trade routes, patrols coming back that'll discover what went on. We need to be gone by then. We'll go west and hope we can find somewhere safe." He took her hand and led her out of the barn.

Her delicate fingers caressed Corvin's hand as they walked. Then, in an open patch of deadgrass, not far from where Duncan had fallen, Corvin stopped.

"What's the matter, my Lord? What have we stopped for?" Natalia said. Corvin heard the cloth fall again as she draped her arms around him, one over his shoulder and the other beneath. She didn't seem to mind that his clothes were damp with blood.

Corvin sighed. His shoulders sagged. He wasn't sure he'd have the energy for this. "I didn't set out to save you from them, child." He ignored her hands massaging his chest; the press of her bare flesh against his back. With a swiftness he'd prepared him-self for since first seeing Natalia's unmarked neck, Corvin spun around and drove his sword through the bare skin of her stomach. "I came to save them from you."

Her scream was human at first, but quickly devolved into something else. Something from the Other Place. Whatever, or wherever the Old Ones had returned from. Corvin wrenched the blade back and forth, sawing up and down, cleaving a hole through the girl's torso.

The wound healed quickly, recovering from the sawing motions as soon as they were made. Natalia's mouth widened as her scream became louder, deeper, more monstrous. The pupils in her eyes split apart, one becoming two, then four in each eyeball.

Then Corvin ripped the sword upwards through the girl's chest and out through her shoulder. He used the momentum of the swing to whip the blade around, cleaving Natalia's head in half across her mouth. The blade lodged in her skull. Her tongue shot out, splitting into four smaller tendrils and wrapping around the blade. Each tendril worked to push the blade out of her head so she could heal, but Corvin kicked her square in the chest. She fell the ground, and Corvin shoved the blade in further.

"Do you remember me?" Corvin said. All the rage and hatred locked inside him for months flooded out. He'd found his quarry. "You should do. After all you've done to me, everything you made me do, you should remember me well. You should have given yourself the mark. That would have hidden you from me. The prisoners knew something was off about you."

The eldritch monster was doing everything it could to free itself. It pushed against the sword, it reached up for Corvin, it caressed its still-human parts to taunt him, but he would not be moved. Keeping the sword pinned in its mouth was the only thing keeping him alive. Remove it and the Natalia-thing would kill him in the next second. Only the element of surprise had gotten him this far.

"Roses in a field of broken glass. That's the dream isn't it? The nightmare you made them suffer. They scratched themselves as they suffered in their sleep and you gorged on their pain. You should have marked yourself too. I admit you'd have had me then. I wouldn't have been able to resist your new form for-ever. Much like the last one you stole." Corvin could feel himself tiring. Exhaustion made his arms heavy. He focused all his hate for the thing and a wave of adrenaline pushed him on. "Did you know I was hunting you? Did you think I was dead? The things you made me do!" Corvin screamed in the beast's face. "My people! My own daughter!"

Suddenly pain exploded in Corvin's mind. His vision went dark as the Lesser One's voice cast straight into his mind; its true voice, scraping across his senses. It was a creature from another plane of existence; it didn't use words as Humans did. Its native language, so alien and unfathomable by the Human mind, had whispered across the infinites of reality. It translated its message to Corvin using the medium of pain, something man could understand. Corvin was in agony. "You have saved nothing, lord of the last day. Their lives and deaths are trite."

His grip on the sword slipped and he felt the creature gain a foothold on its escape. It took all of his will to keep from letting go. Blinded by pain, he forced his weight down on the sword, knowing that in a moment she'd overpower him. He dreaded to think what she would do. He only hoped he'd be quick enough to stab himself in the heart before she got to him. He cried out in pain as the beast continued. "It's too late for you, Corvin. My will is done. You created your own failure in my womb and then you killed it."

Corvin pulled the sword from Natalia's mouth and with the last of his strength, cleaved her head from her neck. The pain in his mind vanished and his sight returned. Both of the severed ends sprouted tendrils of pink meat, each searching for the other, looking to intertwine and reattach, but Corvin expected this. He dragged the head away and proceeded to chop it up into pieces no larger than his finger. With the head gone, the body could no longer sustain itself. Its human disguise dissolved, leaving only the undeterminable creature of many eyes and mouth-like beaks amidst knots of growths and tendrils. The last piece to fade was its hand. That same hand that had so gently guided Corvin to stroke her cheek and removed his pain. Corvin winced as it disappeared and so too did the pain in his shoulder re-emerge.

Natalia. His quarry. The Lesser One he'd hunted, lost, then found again by chance. He'd never known how many forms she'd taken, or why she came to his village in the first place. If the thing had a true name, he didn't care to know what it was.

It was done. The Lesser One was dead.

It was done.

Corvin stopped to catch his breath and lament those he'd killed in order to save them from this creature. They were beyond redemption before he'd arrived. Killing her would not have stopped the dreams. They would have grown inside them like cancer. Their deaths would have been much more prolonged.

But now his pursuit was over. His promise kept. And he realised that killing the thing would not heal his pain. Later he would ponder on the beast's words and find them lacking. The things it had said, the name it had given him meant nothing. Was the message lost in translation? Misinterpreted by a mind incapable of fully deciphering the alien tones? Or was it a foretelling of something larger than himself? The first winds in a cyclone of fate?

At that moment, he did not care. He'd heard enough lies from that monster and they had cost him dearly already. He would not be fooled again.

For now though, now that it was finally done, he allowed himself to weep.

The Lord of the Last Day

THE FOREVER MAN

The Forever Man

The Impossible Storm

Something in the air was wrong.

Corvin halted. His hand moved to the knife at his waist and he listened to the barren forest. Watched. He could sense it all around him, between the gnarled trees, along the cracked tarmac road; a presence he couldn't define. The hairs on the back of his neck prickled as the storm winds blew, billowing his cloak out behind him. It existed within every lash of rain that soaked into his clothes.

Years of protector training had become instinctive. His senses were attuned to danger, to recognise telltale signs, but there was nothing. Nothing moved. Nothing made a sound. There was just the abstract sense in the back of his mind that *something* wasn't right. All around him. In the air. Maybe even the forest itself.

Although he refused to let it show, beneath his heavy brow, he was worried.

He waited.

Then, as Corvin looked up, a chill ran up his spine. Though the storm winds were blowing inland, the treetops all leaned the opposite way, into the wind.

Suddenly the ground shook and the man in black stumbled to one knee as the raindrops froze in the air. They hung there, weightless, gravity's pull on them diminished, twinkling in the dim light before raining back up to the sky.

Corvin grit his teeth. Turning back was the smart choice, but he could smell the salty air from the sea ahead. Water and food were but a mile up the road whereas back was two whole days of nothing. This forest was not what he'd hoped it would be. There were no animals, no edible plants, and barely any sunlight. He'd made a mistake coming here, but now he was trapped by its lack of resources. He stared at the road behind him. For three days he'd not eaten. This forest was enormous. Crippling hunger pains in his gut told him he did not have the strength to make it back. As he stood back up, the ground shook again, reversing the effects of the first tremor. The rain came hurtling down. With a regretful sigh, Corvin made his decision.

There was nothing behind but a slow death. With his hand on the hilt of his knife, he pushed on into the harsh storm.

Further along the road Corvin passed the remains of a town hidden between the trees. The buildings had been melted, transforming the brick houses and the concrete church into slopes of charred slag. Corvin considered searching the ruins for food, but he was wary about stepping off the path and into the thick mist that clung to the soil. The way it crawled and swirled, stretching up with wispy tendrils and avoiding the tarmac road almost intelligently, told Corvin that it was not natural. Like the devastation of the town, it was an after-effect. Some abnormality left over from The Return. Something best left alone.

In fact nothing was natural about this forest. Trees grew in straight rows here and all of them were the same height and the same anaemic grey. Corvin was also aware that before The Return, brick buildings were not built inside forests, so the trees must have appeared after the cataclysm. Did the same force that was making this storm also make the forest? Just what would he find at the end of the path?

As though answering his question, he saw movement on the road ahead.

A blur of tan colours approached fast, running away from the storm. Beneath his black cloak, Corvin drew his knife and the old Glock 17 handgun he'd taken from its previous owner, and stood firmly in the middle of the road, hoping the display of bravado would discourage a fight he was in no shape to finish.

The stranger was raving. He stopped a few paces from the man in black and rested his hands on his knees, "please mister, you have to, to help me," he coughed. Saliva matted in his facial hair.

Corvin aimed the gun at the stranger's torso. He had been fooled by this act before. Though the stranger's eyes were wild and he clutched at a smatter of blood on his shoulder, Corvin retreated. "No."

"Please," the man collapsed to his knees. There was desperation in his eyes. He looked up and saw no emotion in the face beneath that wide-brimmed hat.

"Is this your doing?" Corvin gestured to the storm.

The man shook his head. Coughed into his hand. Blood. "No. It's all him. The prophet."

"The what?"

"He's gone out to the sea. He wouldn't listen. Now we can't get close enough for him to hear us. His storm's going to kill us."

Corvin was intrigued, but refused to show it. Emotions were the lowerer of defences. "Someone's attacking your people?"

"No. I, I don't know anymore. He—" both of them startled as a flash of lightning turned the forest bright green. Above, the pale red sky flashed a sickly yellow as the two colours mixed. The wounded man sobbed, "please save Clara. I'll give you anything you want. Food, shelter, anything."

"It doesn't look like you'll be around long enough to fulfil that promise. Besides, sounds to me like you brought this on yourselves by being too trusting of strangers."

"What do you mean?"

"This person, this prophet. You obviously invited him in, or you'd know if he was attacking you."

"We didn't invite him. He's lives with us at the village. Down by the bay between the cliffs. He's always lived there, even before most of us were born. Are you going to help me or not?" The man snarled in pain and frustration. Corvin braced for the man to rush him. *The gun will be useless then. He'll see that it's empty.*

Corvin circled around the man, keeping the gun trained on him. He knew it was a risk, but he stepped off the road onto the creeping mist. Instantly he felt his legs go numb as the ethereal tendrils coiled around his ankles. The feeling returned when stepped back onto the road, now behind the stranger, but a lingering chill remained in his bones.

"No," Corvin answered the stranger's question.

"Then what are you here for?"

Corvin didn't answer.

"You're going to hurt her aren't you?" The man planted his foot on the ground. Whether he was planning to attack or simply stand up, Corvin couldn't tell, but he didn't wait to find out. He dashed forward, closing the distance in an instant and kicked the stranger's foot from under him. By the time he realised, he was flat on his back and Corvin had retreated back out of reach. The sudden exertion left Corvin panting. But he kept it hidden beneath his cloak.

When lightning flashed again, Corvin realised there had been no thunder for the first one yet. Now he had a name. Prophet was causing the storm. He hoped he wouldn't have to deal with this person. If he could avoid a confrontation, he would. The sea was big enough for both of them to use.

"Tell me something. What is he, a crossbreed? A lesser-one?" Corvin asked.

"I'm not sure."

"Then you're a fool to have trusted it."

"He's a man," the stranger sobbed, "so he claims anyways."

"Then why are you running?"

"The storm's too dangerous. It washed my home right into the sea. I tried to get Clara out, but hers was already sinking. Too close to the waves. I couldn't save her. Please, Clara needs me."

"And who's Clara?"

"My sister. Please. Anything."

"It's not my business. Sorry for your sister, but I can't help. Besides, you won't survive long with that wound. Take consolation in the fact that Prophet won't trouble you no more," Corvin turned his back to the stranger, putting away the empty gun but keeping the knife ready.

"His name isn't prophet, you fool!" The man shouted.

"What is it then?" Corvin said as he started up the path.

"It's God."

Corvin halted, "it's what?"

"His name's God."

Then the thunder came.

A Man Called God

Waves as high as two men battered the village. As one wave retreated, another hit, misting the air with spray. The huts were nailed together from strips of sheet metal and wood, anything the villagers could find and whatever they could use. Since the tide had never come this far up the cove before, they weren't built to withstand such punishment.

Corvin took cover behind the nearest hut. In the distance he saw two figures fleeing from a wave. They reached for each other as the wave crashed like a leaping predator, engulfing them. They were gone when the tide retreated.

Corvin pressed on, weaving between huts, but progress was slow. He was still weak, though his pains were forgotten for the time being, suppressed by adrenaline and a desire to know.

From the sea came a distant rumbling. The water that pounded the village drew back. Far back, past the end of the cliffs, exposing the seabed.

A shadow reared up on the horizon.

The rumbling grew into a deafening roar. The man in black watched with a new kind of dread as a colossal wave rushed towards the bay. He dashed towards a rusted caravan that sat in the sand near the huts and threw his shoulder at the door. It held fast. The ground rumbled as the wave approached. He only had seconds. Its shadow cast over the whole bay. Corvin threw himself at the door again. It gave slightly. Finally he kicked the door in desperation.

The bolt inside broke as the enormous wave struck. Corvin threw himself inside the caravan and shielded his head with his arms. Outside, wood splintered and metal groaned as the huts were destroyed. Screams rang out and then stopped. Water poured into the caravan through the open door and cavities in the metal.

A heavy silence fell.

Corvin heard someone crying. A young girl retreated to the far side of the narrow caravan. Tears marked her face and as Corvin stood up, heavy from exhaustion, he asked she was Clara.

"Don't talk to him, Freya." An old man stepped out from behind her and held up a lantern. He brushed his grey hair from his face, "why you asking? Who are you?" He looked the man in black over, paying particular attention to the ragged armour plating on his shoulders and forearms.

"That doesn't matter. I need to get to-"

"You'll tell me what you want with Clara," the old man grabbed a pitchfork that had fallen off the wall. The instant those sharp points faced Corvin, the man in black had his Glock drawn and aimed at the man's stomach.

"I have her brother." Corvin said. "Come at me with that and you'll never know where he is." His words cut like steel. His eyes were just as forbidding.

"Ben?" The old man gasped. The pitchfork trembled in his hands. He eyed the gun. Though it had fired its last bullet some moons ago, it still served as a diplomacy tool.

"Don't, or I'll put one in you," Corvin said. "I think you've got enough problems as it is. Don't add to them. I'm trying to reach the one who calls himself God. Where is he?" The old man's eyes were weary. Exhaustion wracked his stooped frame. Corvin knew he wouldn't attack. Even if he did he'd be no real threat.

The old man lowered the tip of the pitchfork and sighed, "he lives by the sea. In the double-decker at the end of the beach."

"Is he there now?"

The old man shrugged.

"Is he the storm bringer?" Lightning flashed and wave crashed against the front of the caravan. They were coming frequently again now. "How did he do it?"

"Nobody knows. He does things. He's a prophet, after all."

Corvin didn't know this word they kept using, so the inference meant nothing to him. The old man noticed this and nodded to a plaque hanging on the wall, "you know what that says?"

Corvin took a quick glance, wary in case the old man was trying to lure his attention away. A busted wooden frame hung from a nail and the canvas inside had writing on it. "Of course not."

"It says 'home sweet home'."

"You lie. You didn't read that. Nobody can," Corvin said.

"The prophet told me what it says. He can read," the old man's eyes glinted.

Corvin mind reeled with the revelation. That the metal signs dotted all over the land could still be read by someone... In all his years he'd never known of anyone that could read. The elders who'd survived The Return had been able to, once, but having lost their sight, they were no longer capable. There was no one left to teach it.

Corvin knew this meant something important. What specifically, he didn't know. He would figure that out once he had spoken to God.

"I have to go," he said to the old man. Then, as the next wave retreated, he ran out of the caravan and made for the double-decker at the far end of the beach.

Freya was crying in the corner. She wanted the storm to stop. The old man put his arm around her shoulder.

"Don't worry, sweetheart. He won't make it to God. The storm will see to that."

50

The closer he got to the sea, the stronger the waves became. Each one kicked Corvin's legs from under him and pushed him back up the beach. He struggled to keep moving forwards. As he steadied himself in preparation for the next wave, he heard a voice cry out in the distance. Corvin turned, but struggled to see through the mist. All he could see was the hazy shape of a caravan sinking into the sand at one end. Corvin watched as a shape climbed out of it. The figure had long hair and a short frame and after hauling itself out of the deluge, it stared at the man in black.

Then the next wave hit. By the time Corvin was on his feet again, the figure was gone.

He carried on.

At last Corvin reached the double-decker. His heart slammed against his ribs and he was blinded by the saltwater, but the bus was empty. Had the old man lied? As he thought about what to do next, he saw the waves were drawing back out again. The air felt thick. The distant rumbling out at sea told him what was coming.

Another shadow reared up through the mist.

There was no avoiding it here. He was at the bottom of the cove. Tall cliffs of vertical white rock stretched at either side of him. The rusted bus he'd fought so hard to reach was full of holes and broken windows. It was no shelter at all. He would never make it back to the caravan in time either. This one would kill him for sure. He would never find his answers.

Then he saw something that stopped him dead. He couldn't believe what he was seeing. There was a lone figure was standing in the water.

No, not *in* the water, Corvin realised, but *on* it. The figure stood on the surface like it was solid land. Its back was turned defiantly to the oncoming tide, facing the cove, arms stretched up toward the cliffs.

An ear-splitting crack erupted from the cliffs. The tremor sent a shockwave that sliced though the air as two enormous boulders, entire sides of each cliff, ripped free from the land. They did not fall down into the sea as Corvin expected, but levitated, rotating slowly. Corvin watched, aghast with fear and awe as the boulders met in the centre over the bay and held fast over the water. And directly beneath them was the figure, arms up, guiding them into position.

Corvin was terrified. The raw power possessed by this being was immense. Of all the things he'd witnessed, all that he'd been told about the world before The Return, he knew that this was something truly impossible.

Fear and awe.

The wave was almost upon him.

He ran towards the figure, "God!" He yelled, stopping by the edge of the water, "God, hear me!" But the being was fixated on the two boulders. The wave was deafening. Its shadow was right on top of him. Corvin collapsed to his knees and braced for the wave. "Please hear me," he whispered.

The being's head turned and suddenly the great wave lost its momentum. Its crest broke and flattening out instead of crashing, rushing in to fill the cove. The former protector was powerless to stop himself being dragged by the wave. By the time he came to rest further up the cove, the sea returned to a gentle to and fro. The clouds dissipated and the sky's natural pale red returned. The man called God limped along the surface of the water. He hunched over, coughing from exertion. Above the bay, the boulders still hung in the air, revolving slowly.

Corvin rose to his knees as the man neared. He moved a hand to his knife, but was too weak to even draw it.

"You won't be needing that, Corvin. You'll find no threat from me," the creature said before collapsing onto the sand. Corvin was confused. Ben had said that God was a man. What lay before him on the sand was anything but.

THEY FEAR WHAT THEY DON'T UNDERSTAND

The creature would drown if Corvin left it lying there on the sand. Leaning over it however, he was hesitant to touch its flesh. Whatever afflicted it was like nothing he'd ever seen. Corvin untied his black cloak and wrapped the prophet up in it, then dragged him over to the double-decker.

Brushing back the tarpaulin over the entrance, Corvin saw that the bus had been the creature's home for some time. The metal seats had been ripped out and replaced with worn furniture and cuts of carpet. Corvin dumped the unconscious creature on the gangway and retied his cloak around his shoulders. Then, without getting too close, he examined the man they called God.

His flesh seemed to warp and change. Some areas were wrinkled with age while others were young and supple. When he'd collapsed on the beach his neck was a normal shade of pink, but now Corvin watched fresh nerves grow underneath the foetal skin. Thick brown clumps of hair matted in with grey. The skin on his leg was black with putrescence, eating away the shin right down to the bone.

Corvin was as horrified as he was intrigued. This creature seemed to be living every stage of its lifespan at once. During his years as a protector Corvin had seen all shapes of crossbreeds and lesser-ones; he'd witnessed the birth of a living nightmare and had single-handedly fended off a brood of skin-dwellers; all number of phenomena he could not explain, but this was different. A sense of gravity emanated from its presence. After seeing what the prophet could do, Corvin knew he was out of his depth.

"Impossible."

Corvin had questions. Did this creature really have the answers?

Despite him trying, the prophet would not rouse from unconsciousness. Corvin decided to come back later. There was more to be discovered at this village and the prophet would be safe now that the waves had stopped.

He made his way back up the cove. Past the sunken caravan was a beached canal boat and further up the sandy slope was the main village. A couple of the huts had survived the storm, but most were in complete ruins. Corvin heard weeping.

The villagers watched him, their faces sombre as they recovered their wounded and searched the detritus for theie dead. Freya came dashing out of the caravan he'd taken cover in. She extended her arms and the man in black tensed as she wrapped around his leg, thanking him for stopping that terrible storm. The villagers stared.

"Freya, get away from him now," the old man dragged the girl away. "So what have you done with him then?"

"He passed out. I put him in the double-decker," Corvin said.

"Not God, you fool. Ben," the old man said loud enough for the village to hear, "this man has Ben somewhere! Told me so himself!"

The villagers whispered. Corvin realised he'd forgotten about the man in the forest. He was about to tell the old man when something metal pressed against the back of his head. He stiffened as a hammer clicked back.

"Tell me where my brother is, or you'll wish the storm had killed you," the voice behind him said.

Corvin slowly turned around, "so you must be Clara." Though he'd only seen a silhouette in the mist, he recognised her as the one escaping from the sunken caravan. She stood at shoulder height, with broad shoulders and a steady hand that held the gun. Her damp brown hair clung to the tanned skin of her neck. While her denim clothes were soaking wet, the way her eyebrows crushed into a tight frown told him she wasn't joking about killing him.

"Your brother's in the forest, last I saw him. He found me. Asked me to come here and save you, but it looked to me like you didn't need saving."

"What were you doing in our forest in the first place?" She hissed through clenched teeth.

"The coast has food and water."

Clara pushed the handgun into his temple, "is he alive?"

"Alive, yes. He was hurt when I last saw him, but not by me. About a mile up the path."

With a nod from Clara, two of the villagers ran toward the forest to rescue him. Clara retracted the gun from the stranger's head, but kept it aimed at his chest. She sensed danger in the man's sunken eyes and blank demeanour. The way he held her gaze and spoke so callously perturbed her. She was taking no risks, "you got him to stop the storm?"

"Seems so," the man in black also looked the woman over. There was a sureness to her. Every movement she made was deliberate. As he lowered his arms to his sides, she raised the gun back to his head. The business end of the barrel never wavered from him once.

They stared at each other, each sizing the other up.

"You got a name?" Clara said.

"Yeah." Corvin replied, blankly.

"Tell me it."

"Why?"

"Because if you don't, this will go off in your head."

Corvin's lip crooked into a smirk, "it's Corvin."

"Funny name."

"Funny world. I'm not from round here."

"Where you from?"

"Doesn't matter. It's not there anymore."

Clara paused, trying to figure him out. "How'd you get him to stop the storm?"

Corvin was getting irritated, but he didn't let it show. "He knew my name. But he passed out before I could ask how. I'd like to know how he knows me." Exhaustion and hunger pains were reawakening. His stomach cramped up like a solid kick to the gut and he doubled over. Clara jumped back.

"What is it?" Clara's finger teased the trigger.

Corvin clenched his teeth, "food. Water. Had neither for days."

Clara eyed the old man, "Berem, fetch something." The old man disappeared into his caravan and returned with a plastic bottle of clear water and a few strips of dried fish. Corvin ate them in down seconds and asked for more.

"That depends on how Ben comes back," Clara said.

Corvin's weapons were confiscated. When Ben was brought back unconscious, but alive, Clara allowed Corvin a few more scraps of fish jerky and water. Then she headed off to the canal boat to see to her brother. Berem was left in charge. Corvin's knife and gun now rested in the old man's hands. He sat perched on a nearby rock, turning the scratched old handgun over.

As a thank you for stopping the storm, a woman called Heleena offered Corvin some dry clothes and even offered to hang his black garb by the fire a few of the others were building. Corvin was reluctant to hand his protector's clothing over. He'd made the armour plating on the shoulders and forearms and knitted them into the material himself back at his home village. They were all he had left of that old life. But the storm had left them soaked through and heavy and they stank of saltwater. In that regard he was glad to take them off.

As he changed, Heleena was bemused by a hole that had been punched in one of the shoulder plates, but when she saw a similar circular scar on Corvin's shoulder she understood. He caught her looking at it. "Had worse," he said as he put on the yellow rags that Heleena had given him. She didn't want to ask. She left with his black clothes. Corvin kept a watchful eye on her as she hung them up. The rags were too small for him, but they were dry at least. He soon felt warmth returning to his skin.

Though he was a prisoner, he took the opportunity to rest. The hunger pains had dissipated, but the storm had left him drained. Sleep was the only thing that would remedy it, but sleeping amidst these people was far too dangerous. More than once he'd caught some of the villagers glaring at him, a mix of fear, confusion, and distrust in their eyes. It would only take one of them to turn to anger. Then they'd be a mob.

He rested against the wall of Berem's rusted caravan while he took in the fresh air and listened to the tide flowing rhythmically in and out.

Freya watched the stranger with unabashed curiosity. She had never seen anyone from outside the village before. Until today she didn't know such a thing existed. His clothes were like the night sky and the way he talked was like no one else. He was so *different*. The way he came out of nowhere and stopped that storm... She didn't know the word 'magical', but she felt it on the tip of her tongue.

She needed to know more.

But every time she approached, Berem barked at

her to leave. So she watched from a distance, hiding behind piles of rubble and peeking. Waiting. Curious to see what the stranger would do next. His eyes were closed and his chest rose and fell rhythmically. He's gone to sleep, she thought, smiling at her good fortune. Now I just need daddy to go away for a minute.

The wait was unbearable, but her patience paid off. Berem became distracted by a collapsing roof. As the old man rushed over to help, she sneaked up to the stranger.

"I know you're there," Corvin's eyes opened.

"Shit," she stamped her foot in the sand, "are you going to stay with us?"

Corvin shook his head.

"Then what are you here for?" She twirled her hair between her fingers.

"I need to speak to your prophet."

"Oh," her thin smile fell, "daddy likes him, because he tells him what those lines on pictures mean. He frightens me though," the girl confided.

Corvin nodded, "I think I understand why. What's your name?"

"Freya. You're called Corvin aren't you?"

"So you were listening? I didn't see you there. Sneaky. I like it."

Her face lit up in a devilish smile.

"Does the prophet frighten everyone here?" Corvin said.

"Um, Clara doesn't like him."

"Is Clara in charge here?"

She bit her lip. She looked around. Her dad was still preoccupied, so she had time, "I think so. She tells people what to do a lot. She gets mad at her brother too. I like him, because he makes shapes in the sand."

"Why does she get mad?"

"The prophet told me her daddy used to be in charge here until he was killed. He said she doesn't want to live here. She wants to go to the other side of the forest," she thought for a moment, "are there more people past the forest?"

"Many more. And not just people I'm afraid."

"What do you mean?"

Corvin picked up a scrap of jerky, "like this. This isn't a person. It was a fish. Do you understand? There are more than just people."

Freya cocked her head to the side, "there's fish?"

Corvin grinned, "no. I'm not explaining it very well. Here," he tossed her the scrap of jerky and she ate it down.

"Do you hurt people?" She said with her mouth full.

"Not if they don't hurt me first."

"Do you kill people?"

He paused. "If I have to."

"How many have you killed?"

Before he could answer, Berem grabbed Freya's arm and dragged her away into the caravan. Corvin heard him yell at her, then he came back out alone.

"sorry about that," the old man said. But Corvin didn't mind her questions. Kids had them. The world was new, undiscovered, and it was for their benefit that they asked now. It would help them learn. Help them survive. But he was glad he didn't have to answer her last one. He didn't want to tell her he'd lost count.

"Berem," Corvin called.

"What?"

"I need to see your prophet. Make sure he's alright."

"Why?"

"I have questions. Besides, don't you want to make sure he's OK?"

The old man looked around, but Clara was nowhere to be seen. He ran his hand through the wisps of grey at the side of his head as he wrestled with himself. Corvin saw his indecision.

"Do you know what's out there, Berem? Past that forest? Have you ever seen it? Look around. Your homes are destroyed. You're wide open to anything the world can throw at you. And those," he nodded at the two great boulders looming against the sky. Above them, the black-scarred sun passed directly between them, casting the sky red, "if he dies, you'll never know what's so important about them, it was worth risking your lives. He knows me. Somehow. I can find out what they're for."

As they stared at the boulders, each of them entranced, the prophet appeared on the beach beneath them. A small, dark speck at this distance, but Corvin could sense the man-thing staring at him. Was this sense the prophet's doing?

"You can feel it, can't you?" Corvin said. "He's calling me." He turned back to the old man. Breaking his gaze from the prophet seemed to awaken Berem from the trance too. "Look, you've got my weapons. I'm unarmed. And it's not as though there's anywhere I can run to. Cliffs on either side. Believe me, I'm in no state to swim around them."

The old man looked down at the heavy old Glock in his hands, then back at Corvin, "go on then. You don't have long. I'll have to come get you soon before she comes back."

Corvin stood up and stretched the stiffness out of his arms and back. As he headed down the cove, he saw Freya spying on him from behind the door of the caravan and shot her a smile that her father did not see. She smiled back.

But as soon as his back was turned, his countenance dropped. Once again he cold, sunken, contemplative.

Corvin had gained much from the old man. Twice Berem had handled his gun and not once had he realised that it was too light to be of any use. It told him two things:

One: that the old man couldn't tell the difference in weight between a loaded gun and an empty one. Either he'd forgotten, or he'd simply never known. By extension, that lack of experience could be applied to the whole village. They hadn't bound his hands or feet, hadn't pushed to get any answers out of him. Sure, Clara had threatened him, and while there was a resolve to her, he doubted she had it in her to actually follow through. She was not cautious enough. None of them were. Living here, in the peace and seclusion the forest afforded them, had dulled their senses to danger. Left them weak. Vulnerable. Exploitable.

Two: that if it became necessary, he could take this village.

QUESTIONS

The carpet was dry, warm. A bonfire on the raised platform at the back of the bus filled the place with a welcomed heat. Corvin sat on a rusted metal seat by the fire opposite to the prophet. The flames cast dancing shadows on the wall behind him.

God picked up a thin grey book from floor beside him and tossed it onto the fire. The paper ignited and crumpled. The flames howled. "So, where do we begin?"

"How do you know my name?" Corvin asked the question that bothered him the most.

"You've asked them about me. Haven't you figured it out yet?"

Corvin folded his arms across his chest, "Ben said you know things."

God smiled. The skin at the sides of his lip split like wet paper, "Ben knows too many things. About his sister mostly. She's all he has left, you know? Her on the other hand... I told her once she'd be in danger if she stayed here, but of course, I knew she wouldn't leave. I've seen it." His voice was softer than his appearance suggested. Though he smiled as he spoke, he stared down at the flames, watching the book burn.

"You know something about me too, don't you?"

The prophet nodded, "I knew you were coming here today."

Corvin's eyes narrowed. He was exposed in these ragged yellow clothes. Vulnerable. "So you conjured that storm to stop me?"

"On the contrary, my boy. I did it to help," God looked at him, then back down at the fire, "as much as I can anyways."

Corvin watched the skin on the man's shoulder wither and flake off. The newly grown flesh underneath became opaque. A tuft of baby-blonde hair grew out, darkened, and within seconds, greyed. Then that new patch of flesh became old, withered, dying.

"Berem said you know what the signs say."

He nodded, "all of them."

"How?"

"Simple. I went to school. I learned—" suddenly the man-thing's head jerked. His neck bulged and his teeth clenched as he spat, "it started with the dreams!" Corvin startled. He leapt up, ready to defend himself, but then the man-thing continued speaking as before, "before you entered the forest you passed a sign. Do you know what it said?"

Corvin was too shaken to answer. His eyes darted around the cramped domicile, looking for anything that indicated a trap. But there was nothing. "What was that?"

"The sign. Didn't you see it? Metal arrows pointing out of a circle? What are you standing up for?"

Corvin was confused. The words stung like a wire into Corvin's eardrums. But no sooner had he decided to demand an explanation for the sudden outburst, the harsh words God said had vanished from memory. Corvin too didn't understand why he was now standing up, or why his inner ear hurt. He sat back down.

"I saw the sign, but you know I don't know what it says. Nobody does. Its lost knowledge. What's your point?"

The prophet folded his arms across his chest triumphantly and the part of his mouth that was fully developed smiled, "it says 'Flamborough. Welcomes careful drivers'. That was the ruins you passed in the woods. The town of Flamborough."

Corvin tried in vain to understand what this meant. The ramifications were too complex. It didn't seem possible. As he went to speak, God snapped his head to one side again, "dreams! Vast, empty space!" The agonised words were like a blade twisting in Corvin's ears, but again, as he recoiled in horror, he forgot them.

"Just who are you really?" Corvin said, itching his ear.

"I'm God, Corvin."

"I don't believe you."

"It doesn't matter what you believe. They believe it. But... It doesn't matter what they believe either really. So few things genuinely matter. Almost nothing, I've come to realise—the same nightmare! All over the world!—besides, why did you rush here with such urgency if you didn't want to meet God? You could have carried on further up to the next beach."

Corvin rested his elbows on his knees and considered his next words carefully. "There was an elder in my village. Karl, his name was. He used to tell stories of a person before the return. One who created the world in just a few days with powers we couldn't understand. Karl talked so many times about how this God would come back one day and restore the world to its former glory.

"Before he died he became a recluse. Not eating, or speaking to anyone unless it was to threaten them. Every night we heard him crying, cursing your name then begging your forgiveness. But neither came. In the end he only had his pain.

Corvin grit his teeth, "and now I find you here, hiding, living in an old bus with these people. You haven't restored anything." The elder's frustration vented through him, "what makes these people so special? Why didn't you save Karl, or my people? Why did you let that monster take their minds? Why did I have to—" Corvin stopped himself. He slumped back in the chair, overcome with grief.

The prophet shook his head, "I'm sorry, but that's not who I am, I'm afraid."

"You said you were God."

"I am God."

"Then do something! Bring it back!"

"I don't have that power I'm afraid."

"But you do have that power. I've seen it."

The forever man sighed, "Corvin, I did not create this world, nor the one before it. I didn't scar the sun and do that to the sky. During that moment, the return as you called it, things changed. Things occurred that no Human was meant to witness. That was why your elder blinded himself, like all the others who survived. Did he tell you that? That he did it to himself?"

Corvin nodded gravely, "so you can't be from before the return. You still have your eyes."

One of the forever man's eyes clouded over with milky white cataracts. He closed it tight when he opened it again, it was clear. The blue pupil were already turning brown. "I saw it all, Corvin. The Old Ones tearing the fabric of existence, the schism. The more I've thought about it since, the more it astounds me that any life survived at all. I looked up at those monstrous titans as they passed by Earth and if they looked back and saw me, they did so with in-difference."

"I know the stories. The Old Ones came, destroyed the world that was, then left."

"Wrong. They merely passed by as you passed by a million grains of sand on your way here. Earth was simply caught in their wake. I doubt they even noticed. It's not like we're so special when you think in broader terms." The prophet could see the confusion on the man's pallid face. He couldn't comprehend the notion that the wracking of the world was merely by-product and not by design. "It's like this, Corvin. Your elder, Karl, did he ever speak of things called good and evil?"

Corvin nodded, "almost every day."

"Right. People from before used to believe in them. There were two sides to everything. One side helps, the other harms. Middle-ground existed, but you had a

hard time convincing people of it. But the Old Ones...
They are older than silly notions like that. And the
worst thing was no one even knew they existed until
the day they appeared. The warnings were ignored and
rationalised. All the telescopes in the world couldn't
see between space. We lived on a placid island of
ignorance."

Though Corvin didn't understand everything the
prophet was saying, his mind reeled. Had the elder lied
or was he just wrong? His God had not saved the world
and now this God couldn't. Was the world Corvin had
been born into just a husk, abandoned like a mal-
formed baby? Corvin asked about the rocks that hung
ominously over the bay.

"They are for another time—restless space!
Empty!—I had to prepare them now, because I
wouldn't have had the strength to create and use them
in one go."

"But why? You almost killed those people?"

"To protect them," his face grew dark, "the end is
coming, Corvin. I've seen it. And although I know it's
fruitless to try a stop it, I still need to. It comes from
over there," he pointed towards the window, at a blank
patch of the horizon on the calm sea.

Corvin's heart sank, "but the end has already been.
That's what Karl used to say."

"And yet you're still here. Humans still walk the
Earth. That doesn't sound like an end to me. More like
a new chapter."

"A new what?"

"Never mind. I've known everything for so long,
Corvin, just once I'd like to cast my hand at fate. The
end will happen though. I've seen it. Sometimes it feels
like it's already happened and I'm just witnessing it in
normal time. There's no edge of the coin for this to play
out. And even though I will fail, I'll still try—animals
fled the cities!"

Corvin regret ever coming here. It was so much to

take in. His questions had multiplied since stepping into the bus and now he doubted the answers even existed.

"Berem's coming." God said. "Be nice to the girl, Corvin. She doesn't deserve it."

The second after he spoke, Berem's voice called from outside, asking Corvin to come out. Clara wanted to speak with him. The forever man nodded. "Go. I need rest. We'll speak again tomorrow, don't worry. You get your answers then."

"You've seen it..." Corvin muttered. The forever man nodded.

Corvin got up and left. The fresh sea air hit him as he stepped out into the bright red sky and he remembered where he was. The insides of his ears hurt.

"Don't mind the ear ache," the old man said. "It happens when you're around him for some reason. I'd say you get used to it, but..."

"Indeed." Corvin said.

"I'm sorry about before. If you hadn't arrived, the storm might not have ended. Thank you. Clara's back from the barge and said she wants a word with you."

"Give me my gun back." Corvin stared at the Glock in Berem's hand. The old man held it back.

"Clara's orders."

Beside the bonfire where the villagers dried their clothes was a deep, narrow pit dug out in the sand. At the bottom was a bed of dried twigs and logs. As they burned they heated up the rock that balanced over the pit. On the flat surface of that rock, a thick brown and red fish sizzled. Where most fish had fins, this one had thin tentacles covered in suckers. Smoke escaped from its flesh and as the fat on the meat crackled, Corvin felt his stomach churn.

Clara had changed into a dry white shirt and brown leather trousers. She looked up and down the poor fitting rags on Corvin and lost none of her opinion of him. Now without his black hat, Clara saw a long dark scar over his hooked nose and his dark, sunken eyes. They had seen much more than she had. She knew this. It irritated her.

"I suppose we should thank you for saving Ben too," Berem said.

Clara got in first, "he hasn't saved anything yet. Ben's in a bad way, no thanks to you. He needs rest. Besides, that's not how Ben described their meeting. What are you still doing here?"

"That's no way to speak to the man who stopped the storm, Clara," Berem said.

A frown silenced the old man and she gave Corvin a perfunctory thanks, "right, you've had your food and water. Your clothes will be dry soon and then you'll be leaving."

"I'm staying for another day at least," Corvin said, "me and your prophet have things to discuss." He looked back down the beach, at the boulders in the sky, revolving slowly. He was more disturbed by them now. The black-scarred sun had passed behind one of them.

"It wasn't a question. You're leaving. I don't care where."

"We have more to discuss. He's your God."

"Doubt he'll be anybody's anything after what he's done. So far we've counted six dead. Still dozens missing. We've decided to make him leave. He can rest up tonight, but we're telling him tomorrow. And you're leaving with him," Clara said.

Corvin looked her over. She hadn't brought her gun. Another sign of her inexperience. "You people can't fend for yourselves."

"Like hell we can't."

"You run from the rain when what you should

really fear is out there. You all clearly have no idea what's beyond the forest, or you'd all be sharper." Remembering God's words about the end; whatever form it took, they weren't prepared for it. This, however, wasn't his concern, because he had no intention of being here when it arrived. He just needed to speak to God one more time. Tomorrow. And Clara wasn't going to get in his way.

The only person with a weapon was Berem.

But it was Corvin's gun. And it was empty.

To prove his point, Corvin rushed the old man. Before Berem or Clara could react, Corvin had snatched his Glock from Berem's hand and twisted his wrist, forcing the old man to his knees. He cried out in pain. Clara froze, stark blank in the face of death as she stared down the gun barrel.

Corvin pulled the trigger. Clara winced. Her whole life shocked away in an instant. The empty click of the hammer proved his point.

Clara trembled. Her heart split in her chest and the terror left her cold. In the twenty-eight years she'd lived in the confines of this beach, she'd never experienced anything like this. In an instant she realised that the stranger was right. She knew nothing of the world. She did not know how to survive it.

None of them did.

"Have I made myself clear?" The former protector took his knife back from the old man's waistband then let go of him. Berem scurried away and tended to his wrist. Clara glared at the man in black. White hot fury burned inside her, but she knew if she attacked him, she would lose. She had a feeling he would not stop after killing her either.

Corvin could see the conflict in her, but there was none in his own. "I'm leaving just as soon as me and God have talked again," he checked her shoulder as he walked past, took his jet black clothes, now dry, down from the line and headed up the slope towards the forest.

The black-scarred sun was descending. The sanguine tide had faded out and Corvin sat, invisible in his black clothes, among the shadows on the edge of the forest. The villagers down in the cove lit torches as they hurried to repair their homes before nightfall. There was some commotion over by the canal barge and further down, the man-thing called God's bus was enveloped in shadow.

Corvin leaned back against a tree, trying to resist the encroaching sleep, but the rhythmic waves of the sea were winning. He was so exhausted he didn't hear the footsteps approaching from his side, but he heard the quick breathing. "I know you're there again."

"Shit," Freya emerged from behind a tree.

"Shouldn't you be asleep?"

"Too frightened."

Corvin nodded, "me too."

The little girl was confused, "What do you have to be scared of?"

Seeing the last rays of the sun shine through the child's long chestnut hair, Corvin was reminded of God's words. *Be nice to the girl, Corvin. She doesn't deserve it.* "Nothing you need worry about. How are you?"

She sat down on the damp soil beside the man in black and crossed her legs the same way he did, "sleepy."

"Bad dreams?"

She nodded as she played with her hair, "How'd you get that scar?"

"If I told you that, you'd have even worse dreams," he saw the excitement spark in her eyes and he realised his mistake. Now she desperately wanted to hear the story. "I fell out of a tree when I was about your age. Hit every branch and then fell into the mud. Thunk."

Freya wrinkled her nose, "that's not scary."

"It is if you're the one falling. Imagine it," he pointed up at the trees, then down at the ground. Freya followed his finger and chuckled. He didn't like lying to her, not after God's plea, but he was trying to be nice. If he told her the truth, it would keep her awake for weeks. The scar on his nose wasn't the only one the infant living nightmare had given him.

"Did you come with someone else?" The girl asked.

"No. There's just me."

"Do you like being alone?"

He didn't answer straight away. "It's just the way it is. I don't think about it much."

Freya's little face creased in thought, "I don't think I'd like to be alone. I'd miss my daddy and Ben."

"Then I hope you never are."

"Did you hurt my dad?" Freya asked. She rolled a ball of soil with the flat of her palm.

"I'm sorry about that. He'll be OK. Clara wasn't listening to me."

"I think he's only pretending you hurt him so people will be nice to him."

Corvin took a deep breath and exhaled slowly. The girl did the same, watching him to make sure she did it properly, "what did the prophet tell you?"

"Nothing yet. He just gave me more questions."

She was disappointed. "He didn't tell you about the lord? I'd hoped he would."

Corvin looked down at the girl, "what lord?"

"He won't tell me. But I heard him telling another person that he was waiting for a lord. Something about a last day. Do you know what a lord is?"

A memory flooded back. It was scant, hazy with the frenzy of battle, reddened by rage, but knew he'd heard that phrase before. At the time he was in so much danger he didn't have chance to think about it. It became forgotten, like so many bad memories that day. But here it was again. Here, of all places, where an impossible creature that called itself God knew unknowable things. Here, that phrase returned.

Another question that needed answering.

"Sorry, Freya. I don't."

AN ALLIANCE FORGED IN DEATH

Corvin jolted awake, lacquered with cold sweat.

The nightmare came as it had every night since he'd destroyed the lesser one. And in that split-second between waking and realising he was awake, he saw it: the writhing mass of eyes and appendages that had disguised itself as a young girl and fed off the night-mares of an entire village.

But even before that, it had fled another. One much further away. But not before taking the form of another woman, before murdering the host and ab-sorbing her flesh, then using it to seduce the woman's lover, the appointed protector of the village. It stole the protector's seed and created an abominate life. Then, discovered, it fled the protector's wrath. It ran long and far, but the protector followed, driven by an insatiable hate, ravenous for revenge, nothing else to live for.

The protector had his revenge, but the nightmares persisted.

The hazy apparition loomed over the fishing village, pushing against the boundary between reality and dreams, sneering at Corvin, the failed protector.

Then it was forgotten, like most aspects of a dream, leaving behind only the imprint of emotion and the knowledge that even though he had destroyed that lesser creature months ago, he still feared it.

The child had gone too. Corvin looked out at those two great boulders that hung in the blank, starless sky, and regretted ever coming here. He thought he understood the world and how to survive it, but here he was lost, directionless, alone. Strange forces were at work and he knew somehow that that ageless being in the bus was the key to them.

A part of him wanted to leave right then. Slip away in the dark and continue alone. But he'd been alone for so long. Freya's question had caught him off-guard. It was true, he never thought about his solitude; the brutal regime that moulded him into the protector had driven out his necessity for companionship. He learned to replace it with self-sufficiency and survival. In many ways, being alone was safer than being with a group. But now that he was asked about it, he thought about it. And now that he thought about it, he was aware of the loneliness that he'd refused to acknowledge since setting out to hunt the lesser one.

The loneliness had acted like a slow poison, seeping in unnoticed and building over time. Weakening his resolve, yet hardening it at the same time. It turned him inwards, away from others, consciously rejecting them, instead choosing the safety and comfort of solitude. The prison of loneliness.

But somehow Freya had broken through it. She had allowed him to see the reclusive creature he had become. Even back in his village, though he lived outside the borders and spent days by himself, he still had her. But now she was dead, and the rest of them were ash.

He hung his head and sighed. Though Corvin had spent most of his life alone, for the first time, he was lonely.

Down in the cove he watched Clara emerge from the lower deck of the canal boat. She dumped a bundle of sheets over the side, then put her hands to her face and sobbed. She stopped when she saw the prophet was standing on the beach, watching her. Clara pointed at him. Though she yelled at him, Corvin was too far away to make it out what she said.

Curious, Corvin stood up, pulled his hat on and made his way down to the village. He used the shadows, the black material of his clothing chosen specifically for this purpose, and remained unseen as he crept towards the canal boat.

"You *knew!*" Clara screamed at the forever man,

"you knew all along this would happen and you did nothing!" Bitterness churned in her words. "You could have told me. I've wasted years in this place and it's all been for nothing. What's any of it been for? You could have told me! Look at you now; you won't lift a finger to help. Do something, you useless bastard!" Clara ran back inside the boat. When she didn't return, Corvin emerged from the shadows. The prophet, still standing in the same spot, looked at him as if to communicate some understanding between them. But there was none on Corvin's end. Realising this, God shook his head, turned away and trudged off to his bus.

Corvin climbed up onto the barge and headed down to the cramped deck below. Ben lay shirtless on a bed of sweat-sodden sheets. He was raving, as before. His skin was anaemic, glistening with sweat. He thrashed his arms and legs, not seeing his sister beside him as she wiped his brow with a soiled cloth. The instant Corvin entered the cabin, his delirium seemed to end. He propped himself up on his elbows, "stranger, you did it. You saved my sister."

Clara glared at the man in black.

"Right," Corvin said.

"I said I'd give you anything. I admit I'm not in any state to do that right now, but my sister says I'll be fit and healthy by the morning. Just name your price."

Corvin glanced at Clara. "I'll be sure to do that just as soon as you're better."

"Clara's been taking good care of me. Me and you should walk the cliffs and talk about building you a home here. It's beautiful up there at sunrise." Ben reached for Clara's hand, "my dear sweet sister, I've decided, your saviour is to stay here with me until he has his own home prepared."

Tears welled in Clara's eyes. She turned away and started folding the dirty sheets. Ben coughed. Blood trickled from his mouth and matted in with his beard, but he didn't seem to notice it. He wheezed. Corvin moved closer and Ben grabbed his hand. It was clammy with sweat, cold, but his grip was surprisingly firm. It wasn't until Corvin saw the glaze in his eyes that he realised why Clara was angry with the prophet.

Ben lay back down, "stranger, I think you'll like living here. In the forest I thought you looked like a man with troubles. It's peaceful here by the water. Nobody bothers us. I think you'll appreciate that. And Clara—my poor baby sister—ever since the mists came from the sea and took our father, she's not been the same."

Corvin turned his gaze to the woman, but she didn't turn around. "I'm sure I'll find peace here," he said, adding to Clara's lies. Suddenly she shouldered past him and out the door. Corvin turned back to Ben, "but you get some rest now. You want to help me build a home, you need to be better. We'll talk more tomorrow."

"Promise?" Ben's voice strained. There wasn't long left.

"Promise."

"Good. What's your name?"

"Corvin."

"I'm Ben. My sister over there is Clara." He pointed to an empty corner of the barge. Ben closed his eyes. He breathed slowly for a while, the wheeze growing worse until it stopped.

Corvin covered Ben's face with the sheet, then left the barge. Clara was nowhere to be seen, so he sat down on the boat's roof and waited for her to return.

As he listened to the tide washing in and out, unseen in the dark, he thought he saw a flicker of light on the horizon. It was the exact spot where the forever man had pointed to earlier. But when he peered again, it was gone. Corvin was uneasy with the idea that the man-creature knew something was coming. Because if God knew that it was irrefutable, but still sought to prevent it like he'd explained, how terrible must it be?

He decided that at sunrise tomorrow he would get his answers, forcefully if he had to, then put his back to this place. He planned to tell Clara this, knowing she would be pleased to hear it.

But Clara never came back.

As the damaged sun rose, turned the sky a deep blood orange, Corvin spied a figure on the cliffs, standing tentatively at the edge. Corvin headed back up the cove, then carefully along the arête that led to the cliff. He made no attempt to conceal himself, and although Clara heard him coming, she did not move from the edge. A sheer drop was one step in front of her. Her jaw was set tight against the dewy morning breeze and her long hair and clothes whipped behind her. A bunch of pebbles were clenched tight in one hand. Corvin expected her to throw them at him as he spoke her name, but instead she hurled them over the cliff and screamed at the red sea. Corvin waited until she was out of breath, then approached as she collapsed onto the bare white rock.

"Finally come to save me have you?" She muttered, "Ben would be so proud. Is he?"

Corvin sat down beside her, "yes."

Clara raised her hands and let them fall, "that's that then. My whole family taken by monsters."

"Your father?"

She frowned, "Ben told you, did he?"

"Only a little."

Clara looked out at the sea. I may as well tell him, she thought, everyone else knows, "a mist came one morning. It carried a voice. Soft. Sweetly spoken. Dad went out to investigate, but he never came back. Then when the mist came over the village, when it passed over our caravan, it had his voice. Something, I just, I knew that it wasn't him. Ben didn't. We were only kids. I had to knock him out to stop him from opening the door and running into it," she swallowed, "we were trapped inside for three days before the mist disappeared. More than once, I had to hurt my own brother to save his life."

"I've heard of it. We called it the shrieking mist. Seen it more than once," Corvin said. He tried to speak softly, but the words came out cold.

She picked up a stone, "ever since, I stayed here to look after him. Now he's gone, so what was it for? I suppose there's nothing keeping me here now."

Corvin was watching the revolving boulder, "if you wanted to leave all this time, why didn't you?"

"Ben wouldn't come with me. I tried. I couldn't exactly leave him. He was..."

"Family." Corvin finished her sentence.

"Helpelss." She made a fist. "He was completely helpless, over-protective, he couldn't do anything for himself. But he'd tell everyone that *he* was the one looking after *me*! His 'baby sister'. I hated it when he called me that. Without me around he'd have only gotten himself killed sooner. We got separated by the yesterday's storm and look what happened," she hurled the stone over the cliff, "it's his own damn fault."

Corvin didn't know what to say. It would all sound meaningless. Though he'd been where she was now, at least he'd been able to pursue revenge. He sighed at his own frustration. "The elders in my village used to say that when someone dies, they continue to exist as memories. In that way, they're not really gone."

"And what do you know about it?" She snapped.

"My village burned to the ground. They're all dead."

"Oh." Clara looked away, her anger derailed by Corvin's honesty, "and your people, do they still exist in your memories?"

"Every morning and night."

"And does that make them real again?"

When he didn't answer, Clara looked at him. Examining his face, she realised that the withdrawn blankness he had worn since arriving was not apathy, as she'd presumed, but loneliness. It was so clear to her now she knew, it did not occur to her that she was incapable of knowing this while Ben was alive. It was innate, kindred knowledge, forbidden to all those who still had connections.

She had told her story, so Corvin felt obliged to do the same. "A thing came. I don't know what you'd call it; one of the lesser things, descended from the Old Ones. If it had a real name, I don't care for what it was. It took my people's dreams and gave them a slow death. Now there's just me," His heart splintered as he recalled certain facts he'd chosen not to tell her. Chiefly, that he'd known the lesser one intimately.

"What did you do?"

His face grew cold as he relived the battle, "I tracked the bastard down and made sure it couldn't do it again."

"You're dangerous, aren't you?"

"What isn't? You live with a creature that can do impossible things. Everything's dangerous. It makes me wonder why any of you stay near it."

"The forest keeps us safe. Every so often someone makes it through, but nothing too troublesome," the way Clara looked down at the ground gave Corvin the sense she was not telling the whole truth.

"Your prophet said the end is coming."

Clara shrugged. She'd had enough of the prophet. Knowing everything and doing nothing; Ben's death wasn't the first. Now that her anchor to this place was gone, she had no reason to concern herself with it, "let him say what he wants. I'm leaving."

"It's dangerous out there, Clara."

"Is it much safer here?"

Corvin looked again at the floating boulders. From

up here they were almost level with them, "I can't tell. He said we'll speak again today. I'll find out more, then I'm leaving too."

Then, Corvin saw that she finally believed him about the dangers out there. From the way she looked at him, he also saw that she didn't intend to travel alone. "I can't guarantee your safety," Corvin said.

"Nothing can. But at least we won't be lonely. I'll pack my things and make myself ready."

As Clara stood up, something over her shoulder caught Corvin's eye. A fine grey haze floated on the horizon. The same as the light he'd seen, it was in the exact spot that God had pointed to. Corvin's heart grew heavy as the portent was confirmed. Something *was* coming. The end. After what Clara had said about her father and the shrieking mists, he decided not to tell her.

Clara paused, "What do you do out there when the full moon comes?"

"The same as you do. I hide."

Clara headed back along the arête and down towards the village while Corvin brooded by the cliff edge, wondering if he'd just made the right decision.

As he debated with himself, the stone earth underneath him began to shudder. Pebbles levitated off the ground. On the beach was the forever man. His skin, translucent, the muscles underneath were the same pale red as the sky. He stared up at the man in black, beckoning him to come.

Now they would have their conversation. Now he would get his answers.

Corvin made sure he had his blade with him.

WHAT A MAN OF FOREVER CAN TELL A MAN OF FATE

His sunken eyes glinted in the firelight. "What do I call you?" Corvin said.

"Names don't mean much to me anymore, boy. Call me what you like."

"I've decided you're not God."

The forever man's lip curled upwards. "How do you know? How can anyone tell another person what they are, or what's to become of them?"

"Because *you've* seen it."

The forever man smiled. "Indeed. I've seen it all. You haven't. Clara and Berem haven't. I am all-knowing, therefore I must be God." He leaned back, satisfied with himself.

"We could debate this for hours."

"We could, but we've not the means to quantify, or prove anything," then, as before, his face twisted in agony—"the stars vanished!" Corvin winced at the stabbing pain in his ear. He still couldn't figure out why it happened.

"That's not good enough," Corvin drew his knife from beneath his cloak and placed his hand on his knee so the creature could see it.

The prophet didn't seem afraid, "you're wasting your time with that, boy. This is not when you kill me."

Corvin was thrown, but remained resolute. He was tired of cryptic answers, "but I can still hurt you. Momentary or not, I can make it last a long time."

"I know you can. I've seen what you're about to do. But first, tell me why you really rushed here in the first place. You said it was to validate the blind old man in your village, but that's not it. Hunger brought you through the forest, but something else brought you to

82

me."

Glancing out the window, Corvin saw that he didn't have time for this. But to get the answers he wanted, he knew he had to play along. "When Ben told me your name, I came because I wanted to see the face Karl spoke so highly of, yes. But more than that, I wanted to know why you destroyed such a perfect world and replaced it with this one. But you say you had nothing to do with it," Corvin sighed.

The ageless creature laughed, "the world before was far from perfect, Corvin. There were too many people for a start. And too many people creates too many problems. The Earth was already dying and it was our own fault. If you ask me, we were destined to end up like this, one way or another. The Old Ones simply speeded up the process. Before the monsters came, we were our own."

Ever since he was a boy, Corvin had struggled to imagine a world with too many people. It seemed like such a fantasy. The elders used to describe the ruined cities as being full of life, all crammed together to form a society based on rules. It sounded idyllic. No cross-breeds, no abnormalities like the fog in the forest, or the deadgrass, no full moon scourge, food and water were in abundance and medicine was available on demand. He remembered how Karl used to smile when he'd talk about something called cake.

All Corvin knew about the ruined cities was why they should be avoided. Now this new, imperfect idea of the pre-return world stained the elders' tales. Corvin didn't know what to think. But, he supposed, it didn't matter either way.

Sensing his dissonance, the forever man continued, "I told you yesterday, I'm not *that* God."

"Then what are you?

The forever man smirked sarcastically, "truthfully, I don't know."

"So why do you call yourself God?"

"Because to them out there, I am one." He could see Corvin was still didn't understand. "I'm certainly more real than the God your elder believed in. Did he ever tell you there was never any proof God existed? Or that they only believed in him, because they chose to? 'Faith' is the word they used for it. Faith. They had 'faith' that God existed, because they had no real way to prove it. And faith is just like any other idea: it's only real so long as people say it is."

A long silence fell as Corvin stared into the flames. When he spoke, it was barely a whisper, "Karl's God was just a story? What for?"

"Hope? Everyone needs something to believe in, Corvin. Maybe that's all God ever was? Besides, there was more than just one God. People believed in all kinds, though I imagine they're all forgotten about now too. Nobody can read the texts, those who know the stories are old. Soon there'll be no one left to talk about them. They'll be dead."

"But you—"

"have played the part those people out there needed me to play. It seemed fitting at the time. I had no other way to explain what happened to me."

"You say you saw the return. You saw it with your eyes and you still have them. You still see. What were you before?" Corvin said.

Fresh skin glistened on the old thing's chest as he tossed a book with black and red stripes on the cover into the fire, "shame, I really liked that one. No point in keeping it, not—the sun ripped open! They emerged!—after today." He sighed. His glare penetrated the man in black. "I've never told anyone what I'm about to tell you, Corvin. Are you ready?"

Corvin braced himself and nodded.

"I was born in nineteen-seventy eight, that's how we measured time then, and for the first forty-two years people called me Clive Hardcastle. I was a brick-layer. I built homes for people and I liked to watch rugby," Clive smiled to himself, remembering, "it was a simple, happy life and I was nobody special. Then what happened, happened."

"But what did you see?" Corvin asked.

"Such beautiful things," Clive's face darkened, "and terrible things. I saw all of time at once. The birth of the Universe, then the ageless silence before life's blossom. And then, I saw it all end. All of humanity saw it too. And it burned out their minds. I survived, like those who took their own sight. The pain was, well, at the time it was unbearable. An eternity passed before it receded, but in the grand scheme of things it was probably quite short. Few singular events can be classed as anything really significant, and mine was very short compared to those. When it was over, I opened my eyes to a corroded sky. All around Flamborough were screams and blood, and I had become... This."

Corvin's mouth hung open, "but why you?"

"I've given up asking. Maybe it was God?" He smirked, "I'm an anomaly, I know it. I can feel it; there isn't another like me. But since that day, I've known my entire life, past and future."

"So..."

Clive nodded, "so know when and how I die, yes. And to tell you the truth, I'm not looking forward to it."

Corvin's head pounded as he strained to understand it all. The things the prophet was telling him were things nobody should know. He felt that same sense of gravity in the man's words as he had before. Though he was reluctant to know the answer, Corvin asked about this 'lord' and 'last day' that both Freya and the lesser one he'd hunted had mentioned.

But Clive just shrugged. "That's a phrase that's been echoing through my mind ever since the return. It's more a, a feeling than actual knowledge. I suppose it's a bit like faith," Clive laughed sarcastically, "the lord of the last day is a feeling rather than a straight answer."

"I don't understand."

"I've taken it to mean that some things are still in flux. Not set. The lord of the last day might never come to pass. But then again, it might. Who knows?"

Corvin couldn't help the feeling that Clive was being deliberately cryptic, "I have more questions."

Clive nodded. "I know you do, but you're running out of time. Look," he pointed out the back window at the horizon. The mist was fully visible now. So close that the villagers would see it soon. The shrieking mist was coming, moving against the wind, but guided straight by some alien consciousness.

But there was still time.

"That storm yesterday—"

"Was a counter-balance," Clive explained, "a re-action to the action. Here, I'll show you," he held his youthful arm over the fire, his jaundiced palm open flat. The burning book rose up from the bonfire. Clenching his hand into a fist, the book tore straight down the spine. Corvin didn't understand until he heard the tarpaulin over the entrance tear in two. Corvin understood.

"There's always a balance. It scale depends on the act; I don't have any control over it— Billions dead from madness!—maybe that's also God's work? The action was necessary though. You'll see. You'll understand," Clive explained.

Corvin stared out at the shrieking mists. "Will it kill them?"

"I can't see, but I imagine it will."

Corvin turned to Clive, "you can't see?"

The forever man grinned, but it was forlorn, "I can't see much more of my future. I don't think I have much of one left."

The man in black was confused, "don't you care?"

"Corvin," Clive sighed, "before the return, I had two children. One was nineteen and the other was twelve.

They did not survive the schism. When I found their bodies, I wept for the last time in my life." Silence hung in the air. The fire spat. Wind blew. "I can't remember their faces," he stared off into space, into time, "I haven't been able to recall their names for years."

Corvin nodded solemnly, understanding. Was he still human? Last night Corvin would have said no.

Then singing permeated the air. Soft, affectionate notes glided on the sea winds and both Corvin and Clive looked at each other.

"Time's up. You'd best go, lad."

"I have to find Clara. Our plans to leave have been brought forward."

"I'm so sorry, my boy. I really am."

Corvin left, heart numbed by the forever man's words and the impending danger from the sea. He forced his feelings down deep inside, locking them away where they couldn't interfere with what was to come. Those he must abandon to a grim fate.

THE MADNESS FROM THE SEA

Saccharin wails filled the air as the villagers ran to fetch their children away from the beach. The cloud was enormous, stretching wider than the cliffs. A thick, swirling grey. Those that remembered the last time the mists came screamed.

As the mist touched the floating rocks, Corvin frantically searched the village. Clara was not in her half-sunken home, not in the canal boat, not on the beach, not even in Berem's caravan. He feared the worst. Had she already suffered the same doom as her father? It was true that nobody knew what was inside the shrieking mists, or what happened to those it absorbed, but when Corvin stared at it, cold fear rippled beneath his skin. He did not wish to find out.

The beach was empty as the floating rocks vanished behind the fog. The villagers had barricaded themselves in the few repaired huts with some cramming in several families. All gaps and cracks were sealed to prevent the mist seeping in. Only the man in black was still outside. He climbed up to the cliffs, desperate to find Clara. But he was losing hope.

Then, as he stood on the cliff edge where they'd had their conversation earlier, he saw something that stopped him in his tracks. Impossible, he thought. From this angle high above the bay, he saw an object within the mist. Large, grey, metallic, it moved on top of the water, pulled forward by a large fish-like creature that was harnessed to the hull by thick ropes. It reached the sand. As the metal shape opened up and a horde of people marched out, Corvin shuddered. He realised that he, like the villagers, had been duped.

Things were much worse.

Leading the charge was a crossbreed bound in chains. Bigger than a man, its bare arms and legs were pale and muscular. As it stepped off the metal boat and out of the mist, another figure behind it pulled back his arm lashed the crossbreed with a long black whip. The abomination screamed. Though it had no face; where its nose and eyes should be was a great maw. Teeth like razors jutted out, and a thick tongue almost a metre long undulated as it shrieked in pain. Corvin covered his ears. The shriek it let out was the same song that had masqueraded them as the shrieking mists.

Corvin went prone and crawled around the cliff to get a better look. Behind the crossbreed came a row of humans bearing firearms and blades. They looked strong, lean muscles on show and tattooed skin hardened to the cold sea. The grimace on each of their faces showed their intent.

They came to kill, and they came to enjoy it.

Corvin realised, with dire revelation, that while the villagers had locked themselves away to escape the shrieking mists, all they'd really done was trap themselves for these raiders.

Then, from behind the raiding party, one final figure emerged. Hooded and clad in tattered grey robes so thin they looked empty, it was almost completely concealed apart from its pale feet. The way it moved chilled Corvin's soul as the feet did not walk, but glided over the sand. The longer Corvin watched, he found his gaze kept shifting to something else. It took effort to continue watching the robed creature, as though some force was pushing his attention away. The longer he looked, the more effort it took. He soon lost control when the pain it caused in his temples became too great. What was this thing and how did it possess this unnatural ability?

Whatever it was, this being was a threat he had never witnessed before. Nothing like it had ever been muttered or whispered about in his travels. He had no idea.

He was worried.

A pale hand extended from the robes and pointed its troops forward. The largest raider beat his rippled chest as he unslung a battle rifle from his shoulder, "drep dem alle! Ta med barn! Tvinge ham ut!" He shouted. As the tongued crossbreed was whipped again, releasing its shriek, the raiders descended on the village.

Up on the cliff, Corvin thought frantically about what to do. Then he saw Clara emerging from the forest further up the cliffside. A mound of dry sticks rested against her chest and she stopped dead when she heard the crossbreed's shriek. Her face turned stark white as terrible memories flooded back. The thing that had taken her father had returned.

Then she saw Corvin creeping along the rocks towards her, beckoning with his arm for her to get down. She dropped, and by the time Corvin reached her, she was stone cold.

"It's not the shrieking mists. It's a ruse by raiders," Corvin whispered.

"But—" she trembled.

He took her arm and started north up the cliffside, away from the village, "come on. We have to leave," but she stopped. She shook her arm free.

"They're armed, Clara. Heavily. Your people down there have no weapons and are old. They don't stand a chance, but you and I do. We escape."

"We fight."

"No."

"They have you."

"They're going to die, Clara. I can't stop that."

"You have a weapon."

"This?" Corvin drew his knife. "It's useless. They don't need me making their deaths more prolonged. Because it will. They'll skin that little girl in front of the old man if I try to intervene and fail. Best we can hope is that they die quickly."

90

Clara's eyes welled up at the thought, "I watched you walk into the heart of a storm and force it to stop."

"That's not what happened. He's not a God, Clara. He's just a man who saw too much and it drove him mad. You said so yourself, he's useless."

A scream came from the village. Clara and Corvin turned as a burst of gunfire followed, then more of that guttural speech from the raiders.

"You have to help them, Corvin. If you don't then I won't come with you. I'll go my own way."

Corvin shook his head, "I'm not that person. Now come on," he grabbed her arm, but she fought him. Her wrist twisted in pain as she wrestled free and she instinctively struck him.

As quick as he'd disarmed Berem, Corvin grabbed Clara by the wrist and throat. Her elbow bent as far back as it could as he threatened to crush her windpipe, "you'll be dead within two days," he growled, "you don't know a damn thing about what's out there. You'll wind up eating deadgrass before you know it. You need me more than I need you."

As he released her, he asked himself just how true that last part was. Conscience and self-preservation wrestled in his heart. The road hunting the lesser one had been lonely; the road after had been worse. Despondent, without purpose, would her company fix that?

Clara was more emotionally hurt than physically, but instead of fighting back, she smirked. "You are dangerous. That's what they need. That's what I need. So go and be dangerous."

Corvin scratched his chin.

Heleena scrambled for the filleting knife on the table as the door exploded inwards and a tall raider stooped inside. Her two children screamed as brute smirked at the tiny blade in Heleena's hand. His grin showed off teeth filed into points. She lunged with the knife.

But Heleena was easily disarmed, stunned, and pinned against the wall. "Hvor er profeten? Fortel meg, tispe! Fortell meg før jeg spiser barna dine!" The raider screamed in her face. Heleena cried out. While she didn't understand the brute's words, the way he looked at her two children showed his intent. The two boys were terrified as the raider drew a long black knife with serrations all the way down the blade. Heleena shut her eyes, not wanting to see what he would do next. She flinched as the raider ran his tongue along the scar on her cheek.

There was a choke, a crack, and the sound of something tearing.

She opened her eyes to the man in black standing over the raider's bleeding corpse. His bottom jaw was dislocated and a knife protruded from his throat. Heleena opened her mouth, but Corvin clamped a hand over her and pressed a finger to his lips, "take the children to the forest. Clara's there. Go now," he whispered, emotionless. She left.

Corvin inspected the corpse. It was taller than he was, physically stronger. The tattooed skin was covered with scars, old and new. His clothes were tattered green fatigues and black army boots. A patch with a blue cross and red squares around it was stitched onto the leg. His head was completely shaved but for the long black braid growing out the top.

Corvin had never seen a gun like the raider's. It was smaller than the rifles he'd seen, relics from before the return. The magazine was positioned in front of the grip as opposed to the rear. The stock looked as though it was extendable and Corvin saw it housed a storage slot. When he opened it up, human teeth of varying sizes dropped out onto the sand. Corvin grimaced at the raider's trophies. He looked over the weapon's scratched metalwork and saw that it operated much the same as the ones he'd seen, so he pocketed the raider's spare ammunition and strapped his knife to his waist. The blade was the length of Corvin's arm.

He hid the body and left Heleena's hut.

He stalked between the buildings, over the corpses of villagers until he heard voices coming from Berem's caravan. With the rifle slung over his shoulder and the vicious blade in hand, Corvin approached. A meaty thud came from inside the caravan as metal struck flesh. Freya was crying. Corvin tightened his grip on the blade as he peered around the entrance.

Berem was crawling along the floor. Mumbling. In shock as blood leaked from the stump at the end of his wrist. The two raiders stood over him laughing. The girl cowered in the corner.

Corvin unslung the rifle. He had an idea of what would happen next. As predicted, they followed Berem as he crawled towards the doorway, bringing them closer. The man in black waited until they kicked the Berem in the stomach. Then he made his move.

He dashed inside, thrusting the serrated knife into the closest raider's skull. By the time his companion realised what had happened, she was staring down the barrel end of one of their own weapons, a black-clad protector on the other end.

"Tell me why you're here," Corvin said through gritted teeth, his training and discipline overriding the urge him to shoot.

"Drittsekk!" The raider hissed, "jeg vil spise din lever for dette! Mesteren tar sjelen din!" She spat at Corvin. Blinded by her saliva, she shoved his rifle aside and in the same motion, brought her own up. Bullets erupted from her rifle, deafening in the confined metal space. Corvin, having bluffed to the raider's flank as his gun was knocked away, closed in.

He swung for her tattooed jaw, but his fist stopped

against her cheek. Unphazed, she grabbed Corvin by the throat and returned the blow. She hit so hard he almost blacked out. The metal wall behind him shuddered as she pinned him up against it.

She was strong. Not as muscular as her male counterpart, but equally as fierce. Her fist drove into his ribs and face over and over, opening fresh cuts. He tried to block her attacks, but she was too strong. There was nothing he could do nothing to overpower her. Corvin cried out as her razor teeth dug into his neck and bit down hard. His blood stained her mouth.

In a last desperate attempt, he grabbed her thick braid of hair and pulled her head back until she let go of him. The instant he was free he brought his knee up into her groin, followed with an uppercut, then shoved her away from him.

The room spun, blurring out of focus. He couldn't allow let her to get close to him again.

As she stood up, Corvin grabbed Berem's pitchfork from the wall mount and thrust it into her chest, driving it through her breastbone and pinning her to the caravan wall. The savage choked as blood trickled from her mouth.

Corvin collapsed to his knees. The bite marks on his neck were on fire. He took a cloth from the counter and pressed it against the wound until his blood stuck it on. The bleeding would stop soon. The pain would last for days.

The old man sat nursing his wrist. A pool of blood was growing around him. As Corvin helped tie a tourniquet just below his elbow, Freya, blinded by tears, ran to her protector. She wrapped her arms around Corvin and kissed his cheek. It stung, but he didn't let it show. Corvin told them about Clara and they left for the forest, but from the amount of blood Berem had already lost, he didn't expect to see him again. He collected his rifle and blade and left. He had bigger problems now.

The raiders had heard the gunfire. They were coming.

THE BATTLE OF FLAMBOROUGH HEAD

A hail of bullets shredded the huts as the man in black dashed for cover. Upon reaching Ben's canal boat, the gunfire stopped. His ears were ringing, but he heard the raiders' calls. He didn't need to understand the words to know what they were saying. He knew it too. He had no more cover to run to.

He was trapped.

Somewhere, a whip lashed, followed by a piercing screech and the rattling of chains as the tongue-faced crossbreed was sent after him. Peering over the boat, Corvin saw the beast bounding over the sand towards him. It hefted the rear door of a van in front of it like a shield as it circled around the barge. Corvin saw then that there were only two raiders shooting at him. Where were the rest?

He had mere seconds before the crossbreed was on him. Fighting it while the gunmen were waiting for him to leave cover was suicide. He threw his hat out from the side of the boat by the tiller. As the raiders opened fire on the first sign of movement, Corvin aimed over the roof of the barge and took them out.

Then it was here.

With an unearthly roar, the crossbreed, somehow able to see without eyes, launched the van door at him. Corvin dived to the sand as the slat of metal passed overhead and smashed through the wooden panelling of the barge's broadside, lodging in and looking like a blade sticking out of a body.

Corvin rose to one knee, aimed and pulled the trigger.

The gun clicked.

The protector panicked. He had neither time nor knowledge to fix this foreign gun.

The crossbreed's tongue lashed out. It was thick,

solid muscle. It whipped Corvin across his face and he went down with the force of a swinging kick. The creature growled, drawing a sinister blade with thin hooks protruding from one side. The weapon looked ready to split Corvin in two as the crossbreed swung the blade in an overhead chop. Corvin raised his rifle in defence. The two weapons entangled as the sword cut into the gun and hooked around it.

Corvin kicked out at the crossbreed's groin, not knowing if he would hit anything, but it allowed him time to stand up and draw his own serrated black blade.

Enraged and injured, the crossbreed came at him with pure strength. No deftness to its attacks, no strategy. Its muscled physique overpowered Corvin with every blow, knocking his parries aside before coming around for another of equal force. Left, right, left, right, the creature swung relentlessly.

Meanwhile, Corvin defended himself, waiting for an opening. But he quickly began to tire. His arms pained with every blow they absorbed. His lungs burned.

He couldn't keep this up much longer.

Yellow Saliva dripped from the crossbreed's maw as it went for a sideways slice at Corvin's head. Taking a chance, the man in black closed the distance between them, striking the oncoming blade close to the hilt, deflecting it. The attack came from Corvin's left, so before the crossbreed could bring its next swing around to his right, Corvin whipped his blade over his head in a horizontal slice.

His swing both parried the Crossbreed's predictable attack and cut deep into its tongue. In a snake-like motion, Corvin twisted his blade and pulled it out, sawing through the tongue. Strands of meat clung to the blade's teeth.

The creature dropped its weapon and clutched at its bleeding appendage. Corvin covered his ears from its shriek. It scrambled away, exposing its scarred back, caked with blood clots. The thing looked pitiful now. Mewling like a child. Corvin saw it for what it really was. A prisoner. A bound slave, beaten into their submission. Servitude and pain were probably all it knew. Most crossbreeds had a degree of intelligence; some a great deal of it, but this thing was just a brute. Even if he let it go, it would not know how to survive on its own.

But a protector felt no pity for the enemy. Corvin took up the crossbreed's fearsome blade and finished the job.

The three remaining raiders rallied by the robed one in the middle of the beach.

Corvin, now back amongst the village huts, watched them from his concealed position. The robed one was by its troops. Its presence loomed larger than its physical form. Again, an unknown force compelled Corvin to look away, but he willed himself to keep watch as it reached for something behind it and dragged it into Corvin's view.

Impossible...

It was the little girl. Freya. They'd caught her.

Impossible. They were heading to the forest. I saw them leave...

But it was her. Corvin recognised her cries. She looked around her, confused as though she did not understand how she had appeared on the beach so suddenly, as though the robed one had somehow plucked her from space and brought her here for a purpose.

Then a raider struck her with the back of his hand. The little girl was knocked off her feet, then immediately dragged back up by her arm. Her little face was red with tears. Her eyes scrunched up tight.

Corvin slumped against the hut, overcome as, by

some unknown power, Freya's cries echoed around the cove.

There was no way he could get behind them without being spotted, nor could he bring them closer to him. With nothing but open sand all around them, they had a full turn of clear sight. The ache in Corvin's neck was getting worse. Cuts on his hand and legs were bleeding too. He had done everything he could to try and save these people. But some battles simply couldn't be won.

I can't save her.

"She doesn't deserve it," he whispered to himself. His heart turned to ice.

Out on the sand, the robed one raised its arm. Its fingers contorted into shapes no human hand could produce and its raiders all convulsed. Their mouths opened wide as a voice scraped out of them, "bring me the man who knows all."

Corvin shuddered as he saw the words rattling from a corpse of the man who had lit the fire yesterday. A large hole gaped in his chest.

"Give him to me and no more will be harmed."

These raiders were savages. Driven by a purpose, but still savages. Their word meant nothing.

Be nice to the girl, Corvin.

Without warning, gunfire erupted from the cliff. Corvin peered out at the beach as two raiders ran for cover while the third fell clutching her abdomen. Corvin couldn't see the shooter, but whoever it was had done him a favour. The remaining raiders returned fire as they ran towards the village. Towards him. Corvin readied the crossbreed's sword.

Moments later, screams echoed from the fishing village. As they faded, giving back the sounds of the lapping sea, an object flew through the air. Small but heavy, thrown from the centre of the village. It hit the sand before the robed one with a dull thud. Freya screamed.

If the robed being was fazed by the heads of his minions, decapitated and tied together by their hair, it did not show. Even when Corvin emerged on the beach, bloody sword in one hand and the severed head of the crossbreed in the other, the shape did not move. The hem of its tattered robes swayed with the breeze, but that was all. It raised a hand and again, the dead spoke, "this is your final chance."

Corvin said nothing. His clothes were drenched in blood and beneath them he was etched out of pure, concentrated focus. Aggression, patience, conviction. These were the disciplines of the protector.

Clara emerged behind him having climbed down from the cliff, a raider's rifle in her hand. The remaining villagers followed, scarcely more than a handful of them left. Clara sided up to the man in black and he looked at her with approval.

"Who's saving who now?" She grinned, but Corvin did not speak. His focus was entirely on the robed figure. He poured all of his energy, all of his rage, all of his concentration into wanting to destroy the thing, whatever it was.

From beneath the hood, Corvin could feel the creature's eyes upon him. Its albino hand rose, "you," the dead voices hissed, "much will befall if you continue the path of the living, Corvin."

Clara was horrified at the idea that he and this creature knew each other. But behind his steely mask, Corvin was just as disturbed. He did not know how beings from across the water knew of him. Later this would come to haunt him, along with many other choices made that day.

Clara aimed her rifle at the robed figure, but the bullets went wide and careened off the hull of the raider's ship in the distance. "I don't understand," she said, looking over her gun to see what was wrong with it.

Then the ground shook.

It shook again straight after. The wailing of bending metal followed as a great shape emerged from the mist surrounding the raider's ship. As tall as Berem's caravan was long, its skin was like tree bark and atop its torso where a head should be waved a bulb-like appendage. Tentacles swayed from the bulb and the mist that had disguised the ship exhaled from the many holes in its 'head'. Its great arms were chained across its chest and what was once fingers had fused into calloused clubs. The thing squashed the fish creature tied to the boat that had already died from exhaustion as it stumbled onto the beach. Thick black blood clung to the giant's hoof.

From beneath its hood, Corvin could feel the robed fiend smirking.

Clara emptied the magazine into the giant cross-breed, but the bullets careened off its hide. Only one shot managed to rip through one of its tentacles. It howled and as it began to charge, Clara realised she may have made a mistake. Corvin reloaded her rifle and gave it back. She emptied it again in seconds, but the thing was still coming.

"Move!"

They saw Clive emerge from the caves in the south cliff. He raised his arms towards the twin rocks floating in the sky and Corvin felt the air shudder.

The giant and even the robed one turned to witness one of the boulders crush the raider's ship, while the other was hurled at the giant crossbreed.

There was a deafening crunch as giant's torso ruptured.

Then came a shattering scream. A voice cried and was snuffed out. Corvin's heart splintered as he recalled Clive's lesson about counterbalance. Clara looked on in shock as Freya lay broken on the sand. The villagers cried.

She doesn't deserve it...

The shoulders of the cloaked figure bobbed as it

laughed without a sound.

Then it moved.

With frightening speed, the robed one glided across the sand, making a beeline straight for the forever man. Clara, eyes blurred with the shared melancholy for the girl, raised her rifle and fired. She did not aim directly at her target, but instead a fraction in front of it, so that by the time the bullets arrived, the robed thing was in their pathway. Black blood spurted from the cloth, then it fell to the ground in an empty heap. The figure inside them was gone.

The villagers relaxed, their attackers finally destroyed. A couple of them turned to leave while the rest still grieved the girl. As the wind picked up, the sky flashed green. All eyes turned to their prophet. He had been shot too.

BURDENS

The flesh across his stomach was newborn, soft. The 5.56 round had ripped through it and slashed it open easily. Blood poured between his fingers as he pressed on the wound. The villagers did not rush to help. Instead they backed away, fearful as all lighting flickered around Clive.

The sky dimmed blood red. Waves battered against the cliffs. The wind roared and the trees above the village creaked.

A bolt of green lightning shot down and exploded a driftwood hut. The villagers ran for their lives as splinters rained on them. Corvin watched helpless as a young man fell, crushed under nothing but air. A pocket of intense gravity had formed on that spot.

More spots appeared on the cove, recognisable only by their flattened imprint on the sand. The people avoided them as they fled. Seawater shot straight up in the air like geysers. Some exploded into steam, while some simply hung in the air. If anybody had looked up during the chaos, they would have seen the prophet's twisted face in the clouds above them.

And over near the cave in the south cliff was the forever man, locked in the throes of agony, clutching his wound as all around him, his powers went rampant.

Corvin and Clara made for the cliffs. He ran a few feet in front of her, using his cloak to shield them from splinters. On the beach, more lightning struck the sand, exploding it into the air and crystallising, form-ing unique and deadly shapes. The winds carried Clive's screams.

Corvin crested the north cliff when he realised he was alone. He turned back and saw Clara struggling against the rocky slope. He ran back for her and saw that her ankle was broken, twisted out of shape.

"Stay still! I'll help you up!" He would carry her away from this place if he had to.

Clara reached out for him, but as her hand touched his, she began to convulse. Blood erupted from her mouth and hung in the air. Her eyes went wide, her last sight boring into the eyes of her protector. She said his name. Then the skin bubbled from her bones.

Corvin collapsed, blinded by shock as Clara disintegrated into fragments that danced weightlessly around him. Shock became grief. Then when his already frozen, fractured heart split into pieces, grief became anger.

The forever man levitated inches above the sand, deep in a trance as the tempest swirled around him. He twitched in synch with the lightning. The savage winds drowned out the cries of what villagers remained.

Corvin descended the rocky slope. He climbed over the ruins and skirted around the sinkhole that had opened up in the sand and swallowed the raiders and Freya.

"Clive!" Corvin cried out in hatred, but was eclipsed by the impossible storm. Clive did see him, though there was no recognition in the man-thing's eyes. Lost within himself, his destructive power had consumed him.

Corvin hefted the crossbreed's hooked sword and launched it. Lightning struck the blade as it flew and there was a deafening crackle as it cleaved through flesh that was old and new and split the prophet's torso in a diagonal line. Clive fell. The storm disappeared. As he passed, the forever man's final words carried on the wind.

He had known all along, Corvin realised. For years he had known this was his fate. He saw his own life from beginning to end. He'd apologised for killing Clara and Freya before he'd even done it.

But words wouldn't change the fact that he knew. His apology meant nothing.

The remaining villagers descended from the forest, each of them marked with grief. They would rebuild their homes and maybe one day, a long way off, they would smile again, but this day would weigh in their hearts for the rest of their lives. But they still had each other, those who survived; that they could depend on. When the pain of loss became too great they could share that load and make it easier.

Watching them, Corvin grimaced as that bitter sense of solitude returned. His heart grew cold, turned inwards. He did not wish to see or speak to any of them. He made his way back up the rock slope alone.

"Corvin! Our saviour!" It was Berem. He was climbing up the slope after him. His stump was wrapped in a reddened rag, "Corvin, my boy. Have you seen Freya? She was with me and then she just... disappeared," his eyes were hopeful. Corvin said nothing. He continued up the slope. The old man did not follow.

The failed protector gave one last look at the spot where Clara had died. There was nothing to show that she ever existed and nothing to show how she died. Only memories remained. His memories.

He put his back to the fishing village forever.

That night, miles along the lonely road, Corvin sat alone by his bonfire, wondering if his arrival at that village had been anything but coincidental? A tear marked his cheek and he pondered on Clive's final words.

"The last day, Corvin. It comes!"

The Forever Man

Sam Graham

SHADES OF
OBLIVION

Shades of Oblivion

THE NEEDS OF THE MANY

The boy ran as fast as he could, but the men were gaining on him.

He'd run for half a mile already, out of the barn, through the village and up the dirt track that led to the main road. So far he had managed to keep a good distance from them, but as the path sloped upwards and the boy ran at an incline, his legs began to ache. Each time his sandaled foot struck the ground, pain shot through his shin and threatened to make his leg buckle. If that happened, he knew they'd be on him before he could pick himself back up. If that happened, he knew he'd be dead.

Hiding in the barn was his father's idea. He'd tried to protest, saying it would be safer for them to run and leave the village, but his father grabbed him and shook him. 'No, Peter! This is our home. I practically built this place from scratch and like hell I'm gonna let them force us out. They owe me! I'll talk to them, smooth things over. You just hide in here until I get back. I won't be long, Peter, I promise.'

That was three days ago. Since then his father hadn't come back and Peter had waited in the barn with increasing anxiety. Where was he? What had happened to him?

Peter was no longer sprinting now. His shoulders sagged and his breaths heaved as the muscles in his legs screamed at him to stop. The angry shouts behind him were growing louder, closer, telling him that he didn't know what he was doing, that he was only making things worse. But Peter did know what he was doing. And he knew what they were planning to do too. They'd brought weapons for a reason.

None of them had brought a gun though, it seemed, given that they hadn't shot him, but he knew he couldn't last much longer. He was already struggling to breathe. He told himself that if he could make it to the end of the dirt track he would reach the woods. From there he reckoned he could lose them. Then it would just be a case of slipping away and never coming back.

Never come back... The thought terrified him. He'd never been beyond the woods or even past the end of the dirt track. His father had drilled it in to him to never to go past the dead tree at the end of the road. The stories he'd heard from people—his father, farmers, strangers that came and went—about what was out there had kept him up at night, overthinking every little creak and shadow in the moonlight. His entire life had existed within that village and now he had to leave it. Where he would go and how he would take care of himself were things he would have to discover as he went along, but first he had to escape. First he had to run.

A pitchfork narrowly missed his shoulder and sank into the ground in front of him. He heard one of the men behind him curse. Peter panicked. They were getting too close now. Spurred on by adrenaline, the boy forced himself to go faster, pain or no pain.

He finally reached the tree at the end of the dirt track. He grabbed hold of the bark and swung himself around its trunk, managing to turn left without slowing down. Before he had chance to react however, he ran head first into a huge black shape that appeared in front of him. The boy fell to the ground.

The morning sun was in his eyes as he looked up. All he could make out of the figure was a tall black outline, cloaked and hidden.

The boy struggled to stand. Once he was up he looked over his shoulder. The men, his pursuers, were here. They kept their distance now, their stares alternating between the boy and the stranger. The figure in black didn't move.

"Help me. They're after me." Peter pleaded, tugging on the stranger's black cloak.

Nothing. He didn't move, he didn't even look at him.

"They're going to kill me!" he cried.

Still nothing. Could he even hear him? Was he listening? As one of the men stepped forwards, the boy hid behind the shape. From this angle he could see where the fabric had been patched and resewn time after time.

All four of the men stared the man in black. His long face was covered with a thin black beard. His hair, wet from last night's rain, hung down to his bony cheeks and there was a deep scar visible across his nose. But the men were most encapsulated with his eyes. Two deep, sunken ovals stared back at them, unblinking. They betrayed no hint of emotion or thought. Even though the men were visibly armed and physically built, much more than this stranger was, they saw no sense of threat in him. Those steely eyes stared through them like they weren't even there. It was that stark blankness that kept the men back.

After a moment one of them men carrying a rusty saw stepped forward. "Give us the boy, please."

The man in black moved. The men gripped their weapons, but all the stranger did was look down at the child. Peter's tattered brown clothes were stained with sweat. Tears had drawn lines down his face his cheeks were flushed as red as the sky.

"Don't let them take me," the boy clung onto the shadow's cloak.

"Will you kill him?" The shape said, looking at the man with the saw. His voice was sharp, direct, carrying more command than they'd expected.

The man with the saw spoke for them again: "Have to. Wish we didn't. He's been a good lad has Peter. Would have made a good farmer, but after seeing him run like that I'd have suggested him for hunting instead, but—" he looked down at the ground and muttered something to himself. When he looked back up his eyes were moist—"We're not killers, stranger. Just farmers. We don't want to do this. It was never supposed to happen. Come on, all you have to do is walk on. There's a place along that road that makes beer. You should try it. Just carry on your way and forget you ever saw this. You don't want to live with this. Come on, it's best for everyone." The other three men hefted their weapons. A couple of axes and a shovel with a corner broken off. All covered in rust and barely sharp. Nothing special.

The man in black looked down at the boy again. Peter wiped his cheeks on the stranger's cloak and as the soft wind stopped for a moment, his sobs were the only sound. When the boy looked at the one carrying the rusty saw, the man looked elsewhere.

"Please help me," Peter begged the stranger, tugging at his cloak again. Since he had stopped running, his legs had turned soft. He doubted he would be able to run again. The pain in his lungs was so heavy that he would have collapsed by now if he wasn't holding on to the stranger. He pleaded again. "Please, I don't want to die." But the man in black did not react.

"What is he, a crossbreed? Marked by the Void Rain?" Beneath his black cloak, unnoticed by those around him, the stranger unhooked a crowbar that hung from his belt and gripped it tight. He saw that the leader of the group was confused by his question.

"No, no, none of that," the farmer said in a sombre tone, "he's just a boy. He was checked for the Void mark at birth. I should know, I delivered him. Always been good friends with his father, I have. Well, I doubt I am after this."

"So why are you after him?" The man in black said. Behind him, the child whimpered.

The farmer sighed. "Three nights ago, he was touched by the scourge."

Without hesitation, man in black grabbed the boy

by his clothes, lifted him off the ground and threw him towards the men. Peter screamed. The man in black walked on, not looking back as he turned onto the dirt road and headed towards the village.

The screams ceased before he was half way.

THE OFFER

Corvin sat brooding in the dim corner of the empty pub. Outside was as dreary as it was indoors. He was contemplating whether he should trade some more jerky for another beer when a figure wrapped in a brown cloak walked in and sat down at the opposite side of his table.

"You got a name?" The woman beneath the cloak said.

"Only if you have."

"I do."

"Then so do I." Corvin lifted the porcelain bowl from the table and sipped his beer. He grimaced at the taste. It was bitter and warm, but there was no clean water around for miles.

"It's Asha."

"Oh." He hadn't lifted his gaze since she sat down. He stared at the small bundle of twigs that burned in a metal bowl on the table. They had been burning since he arrived and had not worn down at all.

"Where you going?" She said.

The man in black shrugged, "Nowhere. Somewhere. One direction's as good as another really."

"Where you come from?" She asked.

"East. The coast."

The flames in the bowls on the tables flickered as door opened and someone entered, letting a draught in. For a brief flash, he saw her face beneath the robe.

"How did it happen?" He said.

"What?"

"The eye."

She sighed and pulled her hood back. Scar tissue on her cheekbone had fused the eyelid shut. A thin silver scar traced across her forehead, over the eye and down to her cheek in a hook shape. "None of your business. What about yours?" She nodded to the dark scar across his nose.

"You wouldn't believe me."

She leaned back in her chair, "try me." Her lip curled up at the side.

"An infant living nightmare."

She swore.

"Told you," he said. "Did you sit there for a reason?"

"Looking for help with a job."

"You can't manage it on your own? Companions are a weakness. If you can't do something on your own, you shouldn't do it at all," he said, speaking the words like a mantra.

"It's a two man job. The last guy wasn't good enough." Asha said. The way her voice trailed off told Corvin the last guy was no longer around to argue.

"Why me?"

"You look like you can handle yourself."

The former protector said nothing at first. Then: "I'm listening."

"A fear eater."

Corvin laughed, "good luck."

"Exactly why it's a two-person job."

"What's in it for you?"

"Food and shelter. I do this, I get a place of my own here."

"And what would be in it for me?"

Asha paused. "There's some space for a house to be built not far from here. It's yours."

"You've got that in the contract too?"

"I told 'em it's a two-man job."

"And who's 'them'?"

"This whole village. This fear eater's been plaguing them since who knows when, but they've only recently found out. The way they tell it, it targets the kids, so it's been chalked up to just kids having nightmares. It doesn't take them straight away. Its smart. Only three kids have gone missing this year." Corvin raised an

115

eyebrow. "See. That's not enough to raise attention. Who knows how long it's really been going on for?"

"That explains a few things," Corvin said, thinking of the boy he'd met on the road. He emptied the rest of the bowl down his throat. He decided to save what little of his jerky was left in his satchel for the road ahead. He had not come across an edible animal in days and did not know when he might next.

"Want another? It's on me if you're interested?" Asha offered.

"I'm interested."

Asha nodded, then got up and walked over to the bar. She made a point to step around the shadows that cast on the floor. The rugs that the owner had put over to hide them did nothing as they showed through them. They were human shaped, but there were no people around to cause them. They simply existed without the aid of light and form to cast them, unmoving, frozen in whatever pose their creators had last taken. Corvin found himself staring at one nearest to him. Its elbow jutted out to its side like it was leaning against the wall. A sombre pang struck him as he wondered what that person was doing when The Return happened and the skies ripped open and the world they knew ended. Was it happy? Did it have any idea? It looked like it was enjoying itself. It looked like it was oblivious.

The shadows were harmless, as far as anyone knew, but Corvin still preferred to walk around them whenever he could. He'd never thought about why before and he didn't think about it now; They were simply ghosts of the old world. Before The Return. A world now dead. Corvin didn't understand how they existed, but like the unburning twigs, he didn't question the Return anomalies. There was no point.

Asha skirted around the shadows on her way back from the bar with a bowl and a chipped mug frothing over with dark beer in her hands. She sat down and slid the bowl over to Corvin.

"What did you trade him with?" He asked.

"Pencil sharpener and some blank paper. His son likes to draw. What about you?"

"Screwdriver." Corvin lifted his satchel and jangled the tools inside.

"You got any food in there? It's a long trip."

"You said the fear eater was terrorising this village. It shouldn't be too far. They rarely nest far away."

"There's the thing," Asha sighed, "I've asked around and managed to trace the sightings back at least two years. It only comes here in the summer. Summers ending soon. And there haven't been any sightings from the kids in weeks. But I did find what it's been using as a hovel. About a mile away. It's empty. Cleaned out. And a trail heads West. Enough people come through here and from asking them I've managed to pinpoint where it's going."

"And where's that?" Corvin said.

"What, so you can go off and collect the bounty yourself? No."

"Deal's off then."

Asha clenched her fist.

Both of them turned as the door burst open. The sudden draught wafted the fire on the table and a body fell through the entrance and hit the wooded flooring with a thud. He tried to move, to stand up, but his arms gave out and he collapsed in a growing pool of his own blood. A bald man walked in and stood over him, hunched, hard faced. His eyebrows crushed together in anger.

"Where is he!" He screamed. "Show me the one who did it!"

"Who you looking for?" The barman shouted, but he raised his hands and backed off when he saw the length of the blade the bald man pointed at him.

"Keep out of this!" The bald man snarled. Saliva dripped from the side of his mouth. "It's personal."

It was then, as the bloodied man on the floor looked his way, that Corvin recognised him as one of the men from the road earlier. It was the leader. The one with the rusty saw. 'Good friends with his father', he'd said he was. Corvin guessed that was over.

Realising who the bald man was looking for, the man in black poured his beer over the flaming twigs, extinguishing them so that he sat in darkness. Asha was too busy watching the drama, her hood pulled back up, to notice.

"I'm going to kill the bastard!" The bald man raised his sword over his victim on the floor.

When he did not bring the weapon down, Corvin saw the bloodlust in his eyes. A compound of frenzy and grief, tapered with focus. He had killed before. Only experience granted that level of control. Given the chance, he would do what he said.

"What's happened, Cliff?" The barman said with concern.

"I found him on the road," the bald man sobbed. The blade fell to his side. "My Peter. He's dead." He stared at the ground, letting his tears fall onto the shadow he was standing on. "This bastard, my oldest friend, murdered him!" He slashed at the dying man's back. "But he said there was someone else. Some stranger had my Peter and he was the one who encouraged them to kill him. Said he was already torturing Peter when they found him. Said they had to follow the sound of my boy's screams." He wiped his eyes on his sleeve. "So where is he?"

The bald man pulled his victim up off the floor by his back and pointed at Asha, "is that him?"

The farmer looked. Whether or not he really saw anyone, he nodded. The bald man dropped him. The farmer blacked out.

"You." Cliff pointed his sword at the woman, "take off that hood and look me in the eye like you did my son." Before Asha could react, Cliff spotted a shadow moving behind her, "or was it you? This bastard said it was someone in black. Why did you do it?"

The man in black said nothing. Beneath his cloak he grasped his empty Glock 17 pistol. Asha turned around and whispered, "don't."

Corvin ignored her.

The bald man approached until the tip of his blade hung over the table. Fresh blood covered one side. "You killed him. You tortured him!" He cried. His focus was slipping. Revenge was right in front of him and it was making him anxious to get it. The tip of the blade edged closer, inches away from Corvin's cheek. Asha had moved out of the way and was standing back. Cliff was too close for the gun to work as a deterrent now. Beneath his cloak, Corvin switched hands to his crowbar.

"Asha," Corvin said, "I'm in. I'll take the job." The instant the words had left his mouth, he moved. Using the metal bracers stitched into his black shirtsleeves, Corvin knocked Cliff's blade away from him. The former protector rose up, shoving the table aside and swinging the crowbar down onto Cliff's forearm. The bald man cried out as his bones snapped. The sword clattered to the floor. Before Cliff could retreat, the man in black grabbed him by his collar took his legs out from under him.

Corvin grabbed a bowl of undying flame from the nearby table and held Cliff's face over it. The tip of the flames danced inches beneath his eye. He cried out to stop.

Corvin pushed him down another inch. The old man screamed.

"I'm sorry! I'm sorry! Please!"

Corvin did not yell. He did not raise his voice and there was no aggression in his words at all: "did they tell you why they went after the boy?" The bald man mewled. "Did they tell you he was touched by the full moon scourge? Do you know what was going to happen to him? Have you ever seen what they become?"

"Yes!"

"Then remember that when you think of coming after me."

"I won't."

"Say it like you mean it."

"I won't come after you! I mean it!" Corvin could smell his flesh burning. Cliff pleaded until he couldn't speak. His son's voice echoed in his cries. The way they both sobbed for mercy was almost identical. Finally, Corvin threw the bald man to the floor. He picked up Cliff's sword and looked it over. It was too heavy to be of any use to him. Just a clump of metal, pried off a public bench, hammered straight and filed into a blade. Corvin dropped the thing and stepped over the blood-soaked farmer whose lifeless eyes stared, seeing nothing. Corvin left the pub. Asha caught up with him half way along the dirt path.

"Where are you going?" She called. Corvin turned, crowbar ready. He relaxed when he saw it was her. "It's this way," she pointed back towards the village.

Corvin followed her lead. He'd had enough of this place already. The beer sat heavy in his stomach and his tongue tasted bitter. And though he probably meant it at the time, Cliff would come round to the idea of revenge again. Corvin had seen it in the man's eyes. A gnawing vexation. A thirst that would eventually consume him unless satisfied. Corvin knew how revenge worked.

He checked his satchel. The jerky rations would have to hold out until he could kill or barter for more food. Asha marched forward and he followed, not fully understand why he'd agreed to take her on. He could have simply left the village and gone his own way, but what way was that? He'd stumbled upon this village the same way he'd stumbled upon other places since leaving his home. The only reason he'd wound up here at all was because he was taking a long detour around a decaying city that used to be called Leeds. All he'd ever done was pick a direction and walk until he reached something, then did the same again. He had no 'own way' to go anymore. No direction. No purpose. His days as a protector were over. He'd failed. This was just another one of those things, he told himself. And though he didn't admit it, deep down he knew Asha was right.

Hunting a fear eater was not something one did alone.

DEMONS OF THE HEART

The day grew hotter and more humid the longer it went on. Asha took off her robe and tied it around her waist. Beneath it, she wore a leather motorcycle jacket with plating sewn into the elbows and a sculpted plate in the back. White cracks in the crevices showed the leather's age. Her boots were covered in muck and were held together with layer upon layer of silver duct tape. She kept her hair short and as much of her skin covered as possible. The robe, she told Corvin when he'd asked, was not to hide her destroyed eye, but to hide the fact she was a woman.

"I've seen it too many times," she said. "People treat you differently."

"I wouldn't know. I've never been for hire." Corvin said.

"But I presume you know what women are used for?" She said.

"I've seen things."

"Yeah? I've seen worse." Her jaw clenched.

They walked single file. Him behind her. The broken tarmac road was long and the pale red sky was mottled with clouds. At the sides of the road were fields of yellow deadgrass stretching on as far as they could see. The grass swayed gently in the breeze, making it almost serene to look at from this distance. Though neither of them mentioned it, they both heard the grass whispering to them in the back of their minds, urging them to stop and eat it, listing the fears that existed deep within their souls as a reason to give up. Submit. Succumb. Eat.

Moving at a decent pace, they managed to ignore the deadgrass, both aware that they would be safe provided they kept their focus on something else and they were away from the fields before nightfall.

After two more miles the path turned left and joined a motorway. Though he could not read the old signs that hung from metal posts, Corvin recognised where he was. Before The Return it was called the M62. Though glad to be away from the deadgrass, lines of rusted cars filled every lane. Their tyres flattened by decades of rot, their skeletal drivers still sat inside. Their children were still in the back.

The land raised and as they travelled steadily uphill, voices echoed on the wind whenever a strong gust blew. Corvin and Asha ignored them. The wind voices were just remnants—fragments of sentences spoken decades ago, locked in time by some other-worldly distortion from The Return. They weren't real. The voice that cried for help no longer needed it. The one that asked 'why' would never be answered. But there was one wind voice that always made Corvin shudder. It was soft, a little girl sobbing as the sound of churning metal grew louder until the sobs cut off.

"It is true then?" Asha said, turning to face Corvin and walking backwards.

"What?" Corvin snapped out of it.

"That you killed Peter?"

"Doesn't matter. He was touched by the scourge. You know what happens next. We're hunting what happens. He had to be killed before he could become a fear eater. Does it really matter who did it?"

She shrugged, "I don't suppose it does now."

"Do you think I did it?"

Asha shrugged again and turned back round.

After a moment, Corvin said: "What's your story then?"

"I do things like this and people pay me for it. That's all you need to know," Asha said over her shoulder.

"Right." Corvin smirked.

Both of them moved their hand to a weapon and thought that the other didn't notice.

They reached a small wooded area just off the M62, near the ruins of a melted country house as the black-scarred sun began to descend. It was far enough from the deadgrass that they would be safe, so they decided to make camp there for the night. Corvin regretted not trading for some of those unburning twigs from the pub. Last night's rain had left the ground damp and the twigs unfit to start a fire with. Asha pulled a small plastic box from underneath her jacket and used the dry reeds she kept inside to start one before it got dark. It started raining again, but the canopy of trees shielded the fire.

Corvin did not want to sleep around this woman. And though he didn't know it, she thought the same. As she sat down and rested her back against a tree, she unsheathed a heavy looking cleaver and rested it on her thigh. Corvin did the same with his crowbar and pistol after he unslung his satchel and placed it on the ground beside him. He took some of his jerky from the front pocket and caught her looking at it as he ate. When he looked back at her, she looked elsewhere.

"We're going to need more than this if we're hunting a fear eater," Corvin said, biting into the tough, flavourless meat.

She raised her eyebrow, "you got anything in mind?"

"Depends on where we're going exactly. You haven't said."

"The stories I heard from other places down the road just carry on. Seems like the thing uses the motorway as a trapline. So we just head down the line until we reach the end."

Corvin laughed. "Do you know how long the motor-way is? It goes on from one sea to the other almost. The people that hired you set you up to fail."

"I figured."

"But you took the job anyway?"

"I didn't hear much resistance from you either."

"It got me out of a lethal situation. That man would not have let revenge go so easily."

"Ah yes," Asha stared into his sunken eyes. There was nothing in them.

"So you do think I killed that boy." Corvin said.

Her hand moved to her cleaver. "I didn't say anything."

"You don't have to." Corvin leaned back against the tree. "Have you ever seen a fear eater? If you haven't then you're a fool to accept this job. You'll understand by the end." Asha looked away. She started to say something then stopped. Corvin continued, "his own father should have done it."

Asha said nothing. Corvin watched her sigh and stare up at the night sky through a small gap in the canopy. She nodded to herself.

The rain clouds had dispersed, leaving the starless sky blank save for the bright gibbous moon. Tonight they were safe from the full moon scourge, but from the rate the moon had waned, he estimated there would be another full moon tomorrow night, maybe the one after. He swore under his breath.

"We'll need food before anything else. I'm almost out." Corvin said.

Asha nodded.

Corvin had laid still in damp soil for over an hour. He inhaled slowly as to not move his body. Beneath him, he could feel his heart beating slowly against the soil. He stared at the clear patch of dirt straight ahead, dimly illuminated by the embers of the fire. He waited.

Asha waited beside him. She too was staring straight ahead. Her lone eye focused on that single spot beside the tree. In the middle of the small clearing were two sets of blood droplets. One from his hand.

One from hers. Two scents. Twice the temptation. Twice the lure.

They had waited hours. The moon was almost past. What light it did cast did not penetrate the trees and they were, each of them, losing hope, but neither wanted to quit. Moving even an inch might spoil their chances.

Finally something emerged from the bushes. It was a scrawny thing. Old. Its greying fur couldn't hide the fact there wasn't much meat on it. It's long, fuzzy ears turned and it sniffed the air. Cautiously it hopped towards the blood, dragging its two back legs being it. As its jaw clicked open and two large pincers like a beak extended from its mouth, a long tongue covered in tiny suckers snaked out. They patted the drops of blood. Its eyes turned black.

Asha's gaze passed to Corvin. He was staring at something in the clearing, but it wasn't the animal. His hand gripped a length of rope tight. Asha nudged him with her shoulder and he came out of whatever it was. Then he saw the animal.

It wasn't until the animal had sucked up all the blood and its tongue had retracted behind its pincers and its jawbone was clicking into place that Corvin sprang the trap.

He pulled the rope. The animal wailed as the net lifted up from beneath the soil, carrying it off the ground and ensnaring it. Its head turned all the way around, lashing out its long tongue. Corvin worried it may cut the rope and escape, but Asha ran over to it, grabbed the creature by the scruff of its neck and twisted.

"That was easier than expected. Just a shame it took so long" She said.

"It was old." Corvin said as he gathered up his trap, wrapping it up using the length of the rope to tie it in a bundle. The animal had torn some of the strands when it thrashed around, but not enough to render it useless. He could fix it.

The carcass twitched in Asha's hand. She held it upside down by its hind legs, slit its throat with her cleaver and let the blood drain out.

"Do you want to get the fire going again while I strip the meat?" But Corvin was not listening. His attention was locked on the patch of darkness just beyond where they'd laid the trap. He stared straight at something, but when Asha followed his gaze there was nothing there. "Oi!" Asha said. He looked up. "If you want any of this, you'll have to restart the fire."

The meat was lean and brittle. Once it was hung over some chicken wire over the fire, it didn't take long for what little fat there was on it to drip out. Corvin watched the already dark meat darken further as it dried up and shrank. There was not enough to see them through the rest of their journey. Barely enough for one day once shared between two people. Corvin sighed. There were no other animals around. The fact that this scrawny thing had survived long enough to see its own fur turn grey was a sign of that.

Should I turn back, Corvin thought, troubled by what he had seen in the darkness? Leave and let Asha carry on her hunt alone? Did he really want the reward she was offering? A place to build a home, to start afresh? Was that really what he wanted? Wasn't he tired of all this aimless wandering? Now that he thought about it, he didn't really know what possessed him to follow her in the first place. He tried to come up with a conclusion, but he could feel sleep catching up with him. He looked over at Asha as she stretched her arms and yawned. Corvin yawned too. The moon had disappeared and the stars had not shown in the sky since The Return. There was no telling how much of the night was left.

"We should get some rest. Best be moving again before sunrise." He said.

"You try anything while I'm asleep and I'll kill you."

Her lone eye narrowed on him.

Corvin stared back. "Same." He rested his Glock on his thigh and thumbed back the hammer. There hadn't been any bullets in it for months, but you couldn't tell that just by looking.

As Asha leaned into the tree behind her, Corvin saw the tendons in her wrist tense as she clutched her cleaver. Corvin closed his eyes a little, not fully, and listened. Her leathers creaked whenever she moved, so if she went for him in the dark, he would know. It was a long while until he heard Asha's breathing slow to a steady rhythm, but Corvin still could not sleep.

A voice kept him awake. It was not a wind voice, nor was it the voice of someone approaching; the voice was in his mind. A voice he remembered. With it, the memory conjured the image of a little girl with sand in her fair hair and a wry grin.

'Are you going to stay with us? I think he's only pretending to be hurt so people will be nice to him.'

Something heavy rolled over in Corvin's stomach, leaving a sour, hollow feeling inside. He recalled the girl's face as clearly as he recalled her death. But in the moment before that animal had emerged from the darkness, he had seen a little girl wandering through the woods. A girl with sand in her fair hair and a wry grin.

THE NIGHT HUNTERS

Corvin knew something was not right even before he was awake. The brutal years that had sculpted him into an efficient protector had taught him to sleep fast and sleep light. Be ready, even before his eyes opened. Each bruise and broken bone he'd suffered in those days was another lesson learned the hard way. And he had learned fast. Adapt, be alert, or die.

His senses pricked, cutting through the numbness of sleep before he was consciously aware of it, but he laid still. Kept his eyes closed, allowing his other senses to inform him.

From the lack of light filtering through his eyelids, he knew it was still dark. There was a faint smell like wet fur and slime nearby. Breathing too. Not the steady breathing of sleep that Asha was doing; this was like someone intentionally taking shallow breaths to try and keep quiet.

There were at least four of them, Corvin judged, maybe more. He couldn't tell what they were yet, but that would change in a moment.

Close by, the fire spat. The fact that it was still burning meant he hadn't been asleep long. It also meant he had a light source. He also figured it was probably the light which had led them here.

All of this information he had obtained within seconds.

They were here. They stepped through the bushes a few trees over to his right. As soon as he opened his eyes, Corvin would have to size them up immediately. Pinpoint which was either the leader, or the strongest and take them out first, before he became too tired from fighting the others. Kill that one, demoralise the rest. That was how a protector fought. That was how he'd learned. It would not be easy in such dim light, but perhaps he could use Asha as a distraction.

The wet stink grew until burned his nostrils. Something slithered near him. It stopped when it reached his leg. The creature sniffed the air, then continued towards him. Corvin heard the wet, salivary sound of jaws opening, and razor teeth emerging from flesh.

Corvin opened his eyes.

The creature yelped as Corvin slammed his crowbar down on top of its thick neck. He saw it now in the firelight, the abomination. On all fours and small like a dog, its stumpy legs ended with taloned paws. Most of it was covered in fur, but from its neck jutted a thick length of blotched purple flesh, slickened with secretions. Eyes covered this 'head', a number of which burst as the Corvin struck with the crowbar again.

The crossbreed scampered away mewling, dragging its head along the ground.

"Asha!" Corvin shouted. He was wrong about there being four other people. There were six. One stood over Asha. But she was already awake. And like Corvin, she woke alert. Opening her eyes to the shadow looming over her, she attacked without thinking. Her cleaver dug into the man's leg just below his knee. The serrated edge flayed his calf as she rose up, tore it out and whipped the blade into her attacker's throat. He fell not knowing which wound to clutch at.

The other five held their ground, standing just beyond the hue of the firelight. Like shades in the dark, they were only half visible. Their gruff faces grimaced at the two. Flames danced in their eyes.

Corvin held his Glock out so the strangers could see it. His jet black clothing and cloak made him almost invisible against the night. If it wasn't for the bonfire, he would have been a ghost. "What do you want?"

The one nearest, hefting his sledgehammer, spoke up. "Delivering two messages. One, this is for Peter."

Corvin did not react. His only surprise was that the boy's father had managed to arrange this so soon.

"And two?" Corvin said, already tensed, ready to move. He knew what was coming and he knew there was no avoiding it.

Blood.

The second message came from behind the man with the sledgehammer. A harsh snap of tension being released. Corvin bluffed to one side, driven by his training, taking cover behind the tree he'd been sleeping against as the crossbow bolt shot past him and disappeared into the darkness.

Corvin did not wait. They knew he was there and they could easily surround him if he stayed put. He backed further into the shadows, away from the light where it was too dark to see him.

Asha did not wait either. The strangers' attention had been so focused on Corvin that when the bolt fired, she used the opportunity to tear the one closest to her's belly open. Then she too fled into the darkness.

The four remaining attackers fanned out. The rear guard tried to coax their crossbreed dog to go after Corvin, but it was reluctant. Its head hung low on the ground. As the man scooped it up in both arms, its broken bones cracked together inside. The man hurled it in the direction Corvin had disappeared in. In less than a second it had picked up his scent and limped after it. It was too dark to see the abomination coming, but Corvin heard its tiny feet scrabbling, the grinding of bones and the mewing of pain. He held the crowbar up, its pointed bottom facing the ground.

Corvin wanted to wretch as he caught the creature's stink again. It was a smell that hadn't existed before The Return; a scent from beyond the stars, arriving on the unimaginable forms that passed the globe and wracked it beyond repair.

When the smell was at its strongest, the man in

black thrust his crowbar down. He pushed it through the soft tissue until he hit something hard. The creature let out a shriek, then a whimper. As it exhaled its final breath, he felt its long head rest against his boot.

The remaining four men had taken branches from the bonfire and held them up as torches. The man in black watched them as they crept through the woods. They were staying in a group, taking short, calculated steps, peering into the dark around them with wide eyes, hoping to see movement. Corvin skulked from tree to tree, guided to them by the light from their torches. More than once they looked in his direction, but did not see him. The longer this went on, the tenser the men became. He heard them talk about turning back, letting them go. But the one with the sledgehammer said no. He said they had to stick together and assured them that those two bastards would have to come into the light soon.

Beneath his blank mask, Corvin was smirking. They were scared. Good. This was exactly what he wanted.

"There!" One of them cried. From this distance Corvin couldn't see what was happening, but he heard bootsteps running, cries, then the sound of flesh being cut. A heavy thud followed, then more running. The men called out to each other, "get her! After her!" But then descended into confusion as their attacker had vanished again.

Three.

Everyone waited. Just as the men had regained their composure, a cleaver flew from the darkness and buried itself in one of their chests. Corvin changed position and saw the man was not dead however; the cleaver had failed to penetrate his sternum, but from the way he lie writhing on the ground, struggling to breathe, he was no longer a threat.

The man in black listened to the remaining two.

132

The one carrying the sledgehammer and one with shaggy hair. They were busy debating whether or not to pull the cleaver out of their companion's chest, but weren't sure whether it would kill him, or save him.

Though Corvin doubted it, Asha was unarmed now as far as he was aware. He moved closer, using the trees to mask his movements like slats of tangible darkness until he was near the final two torches. They had decided to leave their fallen man for now and come back for him once Peter's killer was dead. Corvin, waited until had turned away, then rushed from the darkness. Stomping his boot down on the throat of the wounded man, he ripped the cleaver free from his chest. Before the other two could react, the protector swung the blade into the nape of the shaggy haired man's neck, severing his spinal column.

Then there was one.

The leader dropped his sledgehammer and fled from the man in black. Off into the woods he ran. Even if he didn't have the torch, the amount of noise he made made him easy to track. He soon became exhausted, so he backed up against a tree and peered into the darkness. The darkness beyond his torch was stifling, almost tangible. He knew they were out there. How could this have happened? All of his friends, dead? Killed in minutes by this man and a woman they had not expected to find. Who were they? What were they? How could they do the things they were doing? Cliff said it would be easy! 'A two-day job at the most! Don't worry, Marcus, nobody will ever find out', Cliff had said.

Marcus gulped. It was then he realised that his torch was dying out. Running and swinging it maniac-ally had caused the branches to fall apart. "No... No, no, no," he whispered as he watched the flame shrink into a dim speck of amber that left a thin trail of smoke as it died out.

He blew the ember, trying to relight it, but it was

too late. The darkness had taken over. It was absolute. He turned his ear, but there was no sound. Only his own breathing, and the blood rushing through his ears at the pulse of his panicked heart.

Then they emerged.

Brandishing a torch, the woman came first. Her face was flecked with his friends' blood. Then his target, the man in black, appeared at his immediate right. He handed the woman the cleaver and pulled a crowbar from his belt.

"Please don't," Marcus said.

"Why? It's what you came to do to us." Corvin said.

"I was paid to! I don't even know who you are!"

"Do you want to know why Cliff hired you to hunt me?"

"No!" Marcus screwed his eyes shut, thinking that if he didn't know, they'd have no need to kill him.

"Tough. You're going to find out. The man who hired you, his son was touched by the full moon scourge. Other men, farmers like yourself, found out and went after the boy. All I did was step aside while they took take care of their own matters." Corvin saw Asha look at him.

Corvin rushed up to the sobbing stranger, barring the crowbar across his throat. The metal was cold. It stank of crossbreed blood. "Would you have let that boy live, knowing what he would become?"

The man shook his head and sweat dripped from his hair. "Please let me go!" His eyes were still shut tight. Cold sweat left dark patches on his clothes around his neck and armpits. His lip was trembling.

"And what will you do if we did?" Asha spoke.

"I'll go back and tell everyone that old bastard lied to us! He'd have got us all killed if you hadn't intervened!"

Corvin believed he was telling the truth. However he also believed that though this man's mind may eventually recover, his ego never would. A bruised ego was a wound that never really healed. Instead it only grew deeper, blacker, suppurating in his mind like a cankerous root. As with Cliff, it would become an obsession. He would come after Corvin again. It was only a matter of time. It was only because he'd spared Cliff that this had happened in the first place. The cycle of revenge was unable to stop on its own; it could only spin on. To stop it, it must be broken.

Corvin turned to Asha. She cast a look back and he saw she was thinking the same thing. But Corvin continued to watch her, perturbed, for in that glance was more than just self-preservation. Perhaps it was the way the dim torch light showed the contours in the scar tissue over her eye, but burning in her face was a hatred Corvin had never seen before. She snarled at the surrendered man like an enraged animal. Her jaw clenched tight, teeth bared, her eye narrowed on her prey.

Such raw hatred couldn't just be for this one man, Corvin presumed. After all, they hadn't even come for her. His instincts were confirmed when, for a brief instant, he saw her staring not at their prisoner, but through him, as though her gaze had drifted back through time to some past event in her life and she was now reliving it. That predatory grimace made Corvin wonder if the rage he was seeing now was constantly burning inside her? Was it only in times of violence that she was able to let it surface? Where and what had created it, he doubted he'd ever know, but he knew what primal hatred felt like. He knew where it came from, where it resided, and what past events fed it. Even if she wasn't aware of it herself, from that look on her face, Corvin could tell it had thrived inside her for a while.

The prisoner choked beneath the iron crowbar pressed against his larynx. Before Corvin could do anything, Asha broke out of her reverie, then she shoved him out of the way and scraped her serrated cleaver across the prisoner's stomach.

It took Marcus a few seconds to register what had happened, but when he saw the blood, the pain followed. His face twisted and his breath caught in his lungs. It was a deep cut, tearing through the layers of fat and muscle. He lurched forward, gasping for breath as blood and offal spewed from the wound. His knees buckled and as he fell, he reached out for Asha. She was unable to get out of the way in time and he fell on her, pinning her to the ground, his thick hands around her throat.

Without even a pause, Asha reached beneath her leather jacket and pulled out a small paring knife that was taped to the skin of her abdomen. She stuck it into the man's side, then around into his kidneys, striking fast, again and again as he choked and bled on her. Finally she managed to lodge the blade in the side of his neck. He went limp, the weight of his large body crushing her. The hot smell of blood filled the air.

Asha shrugged the corpse off to one side and stood up. She wiped the saliva off her face and the blood off her clothes. Corvin, who had stood back, watching, nodded to the knife. "I'd never have thought of that."

She scowled at him, "you'd never need to." She wiped the blade clean on the dead man's clothes and taped it back to her skin.

Corvin yawned. He looked up at the starless sky and wondered how much of the night there was left. He doubted he'd sleep now after all that, but rest was a good idea regardless. As he sat down and rested his back against a tree, Asha tossed the last remaining torch onto the ground for it to burn out.

Before long Corvin's muscles relaxed and he felt sleep encroaching. His mind drifted to the sea and for a moment he could feel the rough, briny wind against his cheek, filled with that unique cold that only the open sea carries. But when something tangible brushed against his face, Corvin's eyes shot open.

In the fading torch light he caught a wisp of wavy brown hair disappearing behind the tree Asha was leaning against. He saw the face. Impossible! It couldn't be—she was dead! Died along with the little girl he'd seen earlier. What was going on?

Then the light burned out. And all was dark.

The failed protector wrapped his cloak around him, letting the cold lump in his stomach turn over.

MISCREANTS

The road stretched on forever, as did the lines of cars in each lane. Time and weather had worn away the paint, rotted tyres and rusted the mechanics underneath. Their seats were full of bones. Though Corvin knew what cars were from stories he'd been told, he wondered where all these people were going on the day that the Old Ones ripped apart the sky? Did they know? Did they have any inkling at all, or did the madness and death strike unawares like a bullet?

By mid-day they had passed beyond the deadgrass fields and now either side of the road was dry, sterile earth. Nothing lived. The wind voices were restless. Asha had said little since last night and Corvin watched her carefully. He could tell she was annoyed about something. She kept muttering under her breath, frowning, sighing. Corvin didn't ask what was bothering her. He had his own troubles.

These things he kept seeing, the little girl with the sandy hair and the woman with brown hair last night. It was not a good sign. Were they visions? They couldn't be. He'd watched both of them die. Apparitions? He'd never heard of such things outside of madness.

Madness...

So that was it then. He was going mad. His inability to save either of them must have infected his mind. How long did he have left, he wondered? When the mind starts to go, everything else follows. He remembered the elders in his home village; with them it started with small things, forgetting names, confusion. Before long they had taken to sitting in silence all day and raving all night.

Would it get worse, or would it stay as it was, as night time hauntings? What else would this madness cause him to see?

A cold shiver touched his spine as he already knew the answer. He daren't bring himself to think it in case his mind made it real. Made *her* real.

They walked in silence, each absorbed in their own demons. It wasn't until they stopped to rest when Corvin noticed something on the road ahead.

"Any idea what that is?" He asked.

Asha shook her head.

It was too far away to tell. From here it was a yellowish smudge on the road, shimmering in the heatwaves that rose from the tarmac. Light from the black-scarred sun glinted off it.

"I'm not standing here waiting for whatever it is to see me," Asha said as she climbed over the metal railing on the side of the road and descended the slope down to the dry earth.

Corvin called to her from the top, "we should take cover and see what it is. There might be something worth salvaging."

She planted her hands on her hips and raised an eyebrow, "and if it turns out to be something we can't deal with?"

"Then we let it pass us by and carry on. You said yourself, the fear eater's at the end of this road." He gestured to the barren plains behind her. "Do you know what's over that way?"

She looked behind her then back Corvin and bit the inside of her lip.

They waited at the bottom of the slope.

Before the thing arrived they checked over their supplies. At first light that morning they had searched the bodies of their attackers and found most of their weapons to be shoddy farming tools that were barely fit for use. Their crossbow however, still had two more bolts, so Corvin had carried it slung over his shoulder since. He had taken some time to figure out how the mechanism worked and now he planted his foot in the metal wrung and pulled the chord back until it clicked. It was no gun, but it would do, he hoped. Only one of the men carried a weapon that took both Corvin and Asha by surprise. Its blade was slightly longer than Corvin's arm and sharpened along one end. So sharp, it cut Corvin's finger as he touched its edge. Likely it used to be a strip of plate steel, or fencing that had been filed into shape with rectangular holes bored into the flat of the blade. It was fitted with a wooden handle and wrapped in leather cord, making it easy to grip. It was lighter than it looked and made a satisfactory whirr as he swung it.

The only other items they had managed to salvage was some dried meat that smelled like that crossbreed dog creature, and small leather pouch stuffed with leaves. Corvin turned his nose up as he remembered how badly they tasted and the waxy residue they left on his teeth. But they would keep him alive, so he stuffed them in his bag too. "I guess they aren't too bad if you wrap them around some meat," he'd told Asha at the time.

"I'm not fussy." She'd replied, putting one in her mouth.

With the crossbow cocked and loaded, he dug the fence blade into the soil and put his crowbar in his bag with their food rations. Asha gripped her cleaver tight as she chewed on a tough sliver of the animal they'd snared.

Then, when the object came close, Corvin and Asha wished they had ran when they had the chance.

It moved on the sounds of anguish and pain. First they heard the moaning, carried ahead by the wind, followed by the metallic jangling of chains. Finally came guttural voices and the sound of skin impacting on skin.

But underneath it all was a faint sound like the shifting of vines. It slithered and strained like rope being pulled in a knot. Corvin heard a voice, whispering, telling him to show himself and let himself be caught, that he was losing his mind and he was already without hope, that his madness would only drive him further and further down until he was nothing but a sobbing invalid. He felt the colour drain from his cheeks and he was cold. He turned to Asha, but her eye was shut tight. She was trembling, mouthing what looked like 'I'm sorry' over and over. A tear fell down her cheek. Corvin wondered just what the voice was whispering to her?

Against his better judgement, the man in black crept up the slope and peered over the edge. He knew these voices to be the deadgrass whispers, but there was none around. He needed to know where it was coming from.

Marching down the road towards him were two rows of bodies. Each one was wrapped head-to-toe in thick ropes of yellow deadgrass. They were corpses, animated by the grass that had grown inside them after it had persuaded them to eat it. From there the deadgrass had rooted itself in their stomachs, killing the host, but not stopping there. After death, it had wormed its way between the strands of muscle, broke its way inside the bones, and finally, grown out of their pores, embalming them until it could move them like a vehicle. The deadgrass zombies shambled forwards, heads and shoulders slumped, their dead eyes staring sightlessly through ruptured irises. A number of them were missing arms and one was missing a head, but in their place grew sickly purple flowers from the stumps. And in their centres, stigma like two white vines waved in the air, emitting that slithering sound that Corvin could hear.

Each of the deadgrass corpses were linked together by a chain around their waists. As they marched, they dragged a truck behind them that moved on its exposed rims. The screeching sound it made as it approached was like a knife turning in Corvin's ears. Only a few flecks of red paint still visible on its bonnet.

Its front grill was knitted with bones.

Crowded around the vehicle were men and children of all ages. Corvin estimated at least fifty of them. At first he thought they were all naked, but then realised their clothes were made from strips of flesh and bone, hanging loose and strung together with nerves, arteries and tendons. Their flesh that was visible between the patches was smeared the same red as the sky.

And then, when the truck came closer into view, Corvin saw what he assumed was their leader.

Sitting proud on a throne of detritus, a tall figure loomed from the back of the pickup truck. From the shape of its tall body, Corvin couldn't tell if it was male or female. Its large hand gripped the roof of the cab and most of its body was covered in human bones, painfully stitched into its own flesh.

Further hiding its identity was the fact that its head was completely obscured. On its shoulders rested the large skull of a creature Corvin was loathed to recognise. Its long jawbone, filled with row after row of serrated teeth, extended down to a point at the cannibal leader's chest. The top of the skull was covered with holes where the creature's many eyes had been, and tiny bumps covered the whole surface where—in life—the beast had been covered with long black spines.

As Corvin stared into those black eye sockets, he absently touched the scar across his nose. It had been years since that rainy night when a newborn living nightmare, less than half the size of the one that skull was from, gave it to him, but he felt it now like it had only just happened. He remembered the cries. Saw the blood on the trees. Burned the remains of those it killed.

Corvin snapped out of it as the truck passed by. Pulled behind it, also in chains, were more people. These were not the animated corpses of deadgrass zombies, but women and children. They were covered with blood and bruises. Their scrawny legs bowed outwards as they staggered along, their ribs and pelvis' protruded from their skin and their heads hung low from exhaustion. Some had fingers missing, some lacked whole hands. From the flesh and bones worn by their captors, Corvin didn't have to guess what had happened to them. He looked back at the truck where the leader sat. There was someone else with them now, but the cannibal leader did not seem to notice. Her head rested on the leader's bone-plated shoulder. Wavy brown hair hung down and troubles marked the edges of her face. She stared at Corvin with the same longing and hope they had in the seconds before she died.

'You're dangerous aren't you? What do you do out there when the full moon comes?'

Clara. Her name was Clara. Corvin heard her voice as clear as he heard the scraping wheels. And the little girl he'd seen last night was Freya. They were both dead. Not by his hand, but by his presence.

Corvin screwed his eyes shut and tried to force the apparition away. The job. Focus on the job at hand. When he opened his eyes the apparition gone, but he could still feel Clara's gaze boring into his soul, leaving a pain like a brick pressing on his chest.

But though the apparition was gone, he saw that there were other eyes staring at him.

A boy. Not very old, one of the prisoners trailing behind the truck. The chain that pulled tight around his wrists and throat extended to the woman beside him. The little finger on his hand was a bloody stump. His desperate eyes met the man in black's and without words, Corvin could feel the child begging for help.

Corvin shook his head, but the child was already breaking away from the line to approach him. His chains rattled as he struggled to free his hands. Two of the tribesmen heard the noise and rushed over. The rest of the prisoners backed away. The tribesmen did not hesitate. With a spear made from sharpened rebar, one of them impaled the boy through the stomach. They didn't bother to unchain him; the rest of the line would simply have to drag the extra weight. Tenderise the meat.

By this point the convoy had stopped. Their leader turned around in its throne to see what was going on. As the boy fell and the two tribesmen threatened the rest of the prisoners with their spears, the leader, satisfied, turned to signal the advance. It was then that the hidden eyes of the cannibal lord met with the former protector's.

Time seemed to halt as they stared at one another. Neither was able to move or look away. Corvin felt his heart thrum against his ribs. He felt the adrenaline begin to surge through his veins. The urge to move reared up within him. Just then, the cannibal lord raised its arm.

Corvin didn't hesitate. He unslung the crossbow, aimed, and fired before the throned figure could shout an order. The bolt hit square in the centre of the living nightmare's skull. The cannibal lord reeled from the impact, but soon recovered. The bone mask was too thick; the crossbow bolt had crumpled on impact. Corvin felt the cannibal lord's fury from beneath that mask.

"What are you doing?" Asha whispered from below, but Corvin ignored her. He planted the crossbow on the ground and pulled the chord back into position. His hands were on fire by the time it clicked and he slid the last arrow into the groove.

By now the whole tribe were watching him, laughing and taunting him. Every single one of them was armed. Some with blades, but most with cudgels fashioned from bones.

Their lord stood tall and proud in the back of the truck. It called out a word that sounded like clearing one's throat. Then, their orders received, the horde ran.

Corvin fired the last bolt and a tribesman fell clutching his heart, then he dumped the crossbow and retreated down the hill. Grabbing the fence blade from the dirt, he saw that Asha was already a quarter the way across the dirt fields. Corvin ran to catch up.

The cannibals screamed in their gutteral language as they chased after him, seeing only a kill and a meal before them. As man in black sprinted, the heavy satchel that hung by his hip kept flinging around and hitting against his leg, slowing him down, so he unslung it and abandoned it. This allowed him to run more streamlined and he soon caught up to Asha when she paused half way across the field to look behind her.

"Keep moving!" Corvin called. She carried on, speeding on ahead while Corvin maintained a steady pace, aiming to spread out his stamina for a long run. And a long run it was. At the end of the field was an old, broken road. The tarmac was cracked. Past cataclysms had raised the road into slats of varying heights. At either side were gnarled husks of dead trees, their brittle branches netted together to form barriers they did not have time to cut through. There was no other way but the road.

Asha was panting. She looked behind her and to her horror, saw the cannibals were gaining. Driven by frenzy and hunger, they had not seemed to tire at all. She looked at Corvin and both felt the same dread running up their spines. Though neither mentioned it, they both decided they would not allow themselves to live as one of their prisoners. If they had to, they would choose death.

Together they ran down the broken road, working as a team, hoisting each other up onto the higher slabs, calling out pitfalls and cracks as they saw them. They hopped and leapt over the slats and pitfalls,

145

dropped down into crevices, squeezed through narrow gaps and climbed up the other sides.

Eventually they came to a dead end where a mound of earth jutted up so high it was higher than both of them combined. The rock surface was too smooth to climb. Hanging off the top were fragments of tarmac where the road continued. They looked around. The walls of trees made going around impossible. They were trapped. They both cursed.

Then an idea struck. Corvin turned his back to the wall and cupped his hands together and gestured for Asha to run to him. Without a second thought, she ran. As her foot planted in Corvin's hand, he lifted, raising her up to the air and using the momentum of her run to throw her. She cried out in pain as her arm pulled, taking all of her weight at once as she gripped the lip of crumbling tarmac at the top. Corvin helped her up by pushing the bottom of her boots. Once over the top, she disappeared. Corvin waited for her to return, but when he turned to see the cannibals were almost on him, he feared that she was not coming back. He drew the fence blade.

"Come on! Take a run up!" Asha appeared over the edge of the road. Her hand reached out for him.

Corvin sighed with relief as he sheathed his weapon. He took a run up and leapt, kicking off the vertical wall of stone to gain an extra few inches, but his grasp fell just short of Asha's hand. He tried again, but the second attempt was worse. He doubled over, panting. Too exhausted now to make a third attempt worthwhile. Behind him he heard the hordes laughing. They were here. Corvin turned to meet them, drawing his blade as they fanned around him.

He weighed up his options.

He could take them one at a time. He was certain of this. These cannibals were wasted by hunger and maddened by whatever toll cannibalism had taken on them. The brutal regime his father had created to shape him into his village's protector had taught him several ways to best them. He knew how to adapt his technique depending on the size and weight of his opponents—to locate a weakness in them early on and exploit it. End it quick. The training was gruelling. Painful. Attacks were sprung on him daily at any point. These were not sparring matches, but life or death. His attackers—people from his village, the same ones he'd known his entire life—were selected at random each day. Their orders were simple: hurt Corvin. For years, every bruise and broken bone he suffered was a lesson learned the hard way. All he had to do was fend off men and women that were much older and stronger than him. After two years of daily assaults, Corvin had become proficient enough at one-on-one combat to not be hurt every day, so in response, the training intensified and two were set on him at a time. This forced him to learn faster than ever before, to adapt quickly. Most of his childhood and teenage nights were spent tearfully nursing his bruises, assuming he would die that night in his sleep, or be killed the very next day. The one time he pleaded his father to stop the training, he would not listen. The training persisted. And Corvin didn't die. So instead he fought.

But even so, Corvin knew his limitations. He could not fight this force. A quick count saw twenty-five of them, all armed. They kept their distance for now, spitting and shouting in their gutteral language, but Corvin knew as soon as he moved, they would swarm him. Tear him to pieces and eat him.

The failed protector had one last idea, and he didn't like it at all.

"Asha! Get ready!"

He ran at the wall again. Before he jumped, he turned the fence blade over in his hand so that he gripped the blade. Leaping, he kicked off the wall and reached up, thrusting the handle above him.

Asha grabbed the leather handle and held tight. Corvin grit his teeth as his weight fell on the hand that clutched the blade. Its sharp edge cut deep into his palm and he slid down the blade as blood trickled from his hand. The protector grimaced as the tip of the blade sliced his wrist.

The pain was unbearable. Corvin's teeth clenched so tight he thought they would break. Every fibre of him told him to let go, stop it from cutting into him. But he held on. The further his hand slipped, the tighter he gripped the steel, widening the gash on his wrist. Below him, the hordes swung their weapons trying to reach him. Above, Asha struggled to hoist him up. She planted both feet into the ground and pulled until her back threatened to give out. Corvin was too blinded by agony to notice being lifted up. Only when he felt Asha's hand grasp his shoulder did he think he might actually make it. He reached with his other arm and gripped the tarmac.

Then he cried out in pain.

Something rammed through the back of his thigh. It pierced the skin and muscle before breaking out through the front of his leg. Corvin's grip failed and he let go. He would have fallen into the cannibal's mercy, but Asha grabbed him and hauled him up the rest of the way. When he was safely on the ledge he looked down and saw a needle-thin length of bone jutting through both sides of his leg. He felt nauseous as he could feel the bone weapon grating the meat inside his leg.

Asha handed him the fence blade. It was dripping with his own blood. His hand and up his forearm was still gushing. His heart pounded and he felt faint. Then he screamed as Asha pulled the bone-needle from his leg, then draped his arm over her shoulder and hauled him to his feet.

"Can you move?" Asha said.

Corvin managed a nod.

"Good. We can't stay here. And I can't leave you. I hired you for a two-man job, remember?"

Corvin didn't hear her.

Below them, the cannibals were forming a human pyramid in order to climb up the ledge.

Corvin sheathed his weapon in his belt and tried to move, but his legs failed. He collapsed, his bloodied hand scraped against the tarmac. He was in so much pain a part of him didn't want to get up and carry on. But again Asha would not let him quit. Time and time again she dragged him to his feet—each time he fell, she picked him up. The wound in his leg was not bleeding, but as he limped he could feel the muscles moving in ways they weren't supposed to. They carried on.

Further along the road they passed something that stopped Corvin in his tracks. Asha, jarred by his sudden halt, stared at him.

"What is it?" She asked, then became worried. For the first time since meeting this man, his eyes showed more than blankness. They were wide open. Terrified.

Corvin swallowed as he stared at the tree stump to his right. It was cut into the shape of a chair with a high backrest. The sudden recognition hit him like a punch in the face—He knew where they were.

How hadn't he realised this entire time? Had he recognised their surroundings back on the road and refused to acknowledge it? Was he too pre-occupied with the cannibals? Or was this just another sign of madness?

He knew where they were. He knew there was a place they could go, but—

"Don't pass out on me, Corvin," Asha shook him, "or I'll dump your ass here for them to eat!" The tone in her voice was enough to keep him conscious.

He could hear the hordes. They had been slowed by the tall ridge, but they were over it now. They were still coming.

What choice did they have? They couldn't keep hobbling down the road like this; the cannibals would catch up to them in minutes. If they were lucky they'd be killed first. Looking at that tree stump, memories flooded back to him. He remembered that the weed-ridden field the chair was facing was actually a bog of deep black mud. Beyond that was a lifeless forest where the sounds of birds still echoed as the branches rattled. Corvin's heart twinged as he recalled a small cave that sat underneath a rock formation in that forest. A stone mound lie at the bottom, like a grave, but it couldn't have been. Corvin wasn't able to save her body.

In the centre of the forest was a settlement. This, Corvin dreaded the most. Asha could see it in his face as clear as she saw the blood on his hand. He could not hide it and he didn't try to either. Though he dreaded going there, he knew there was no other choice. They would be safe there. He knew that village like the back of his hand, every hiding place, every dark corner.

Everyone remembers their home.

Sam Graham

MEMORIES

He could still feel the heat from the flames.
Still smell the blood in the air.
Still hear the screams.

SINS OF THE PAST

The bog was deep. Navigating it took time; it was too vast to go around. Every step had to be precise. Years ago, trial and error had taught Corvin the route, but his memory of the solid patches and rocks just beneath the surface was marred by the screaming pain in his arm and leg. His sight blurred. More than once, as they crossed, his eyes rolled back and he blacked out. If it wasn't for Asha, he'd have sunk to the bottom of the bog.

When they finally reached the opposite bank, Asha dropped Corvin on the ground and collapsed next to him, struggling to breathe. She watched as several cannibals sank into the mud, their arms flailing. They disappeared beneath the surface before their tribes-men could pull them out, and their bodies sank down to the bottom, joining the corpses of traitors and weaklings from Corvin's home village.

One of the cannibals brought up a long branch and prodded the surface of the mud with it until he found the spots of solid earth. He shouted out in their raspy language and the rest stepped where he pointed to. They were crossing the mud.

Asha pushed herself up and kept moving, carrying her half-conscious companion over her shoulder. Her knees threatened to give out. Her lungs burned as Corvin guided her through the forest, leading her to a set of tall iron gates, charred and blackened.

"What the hell?" Asha whispered as she stared at the high wall of metal spikes at either side, pieced together with anything from rebar and machine parts to lawnmower blades.

Corvin muttered something, but Asha didn't hear. She sat him down while she pulled the front gate open. Rust shook from the joints and the metal groaned.

Asha shuddered at what she saw beyond.

Entire structures were constructed from vehicle parts. Walls of panelling, doors, bonnets, held up by steel chassis and frames. They were not large buildings like those in the city ruins, but there were a lot of them. More than Asha cared to count. The mud path led straight through the centre of the village and smaller paths branched off in a ribcage pattern. But the ingenuity of this scrapyard village was not what shocked her. It was the amount of corpses littering the path.

They had decomposed, but shreds of clothing still clung to their bones, covered in green-black mould. Most were not intact; arms and legs were broken, vertebrae were twisted, puncture wounds and blunt force marked the skulls.

This place was a nightmare. Asha's spine tingled as she dared to imagine what had happened. She felt its cold indifference in her stomach. It felt like the touch of death.

Limping up beside her, Corvin closed his eyes to the scene before them, but in blocking out the present, he saw the past. He saw how those corpses had come to lie there. He could have told Asha every single one of their names and described the terror and confusion in their final moments. Some begged him to stop. Some fought back. Most just asked why.

Asha pricked up at the sound of the cannibals moving through the forest. She swore, hoping they would have given up by now, and hurried down the slight incline into the scrapyard. Every one of the buildings was blackened with the same charring as the gates. She even thought she could still smell the flames for a moment. Corvin limped gravely alongside her, beckoning her to follow him. Asha followed.

As the cannibals reached the gates they entered cautiously. They spread out and stalked through the streets, clutching their weapons tight in their hands.

The cracking of bones resounded throughout the village as they stepped through them. The man and the woman they had followed were here somewhere. They could smell them.

Huddled inside a tiny hut made from bus and tractor parts, Asha and Corvin sat frozen as a line of cannibals passed by outside. She stiffened, her hand going for her weapon, but the hut was disguised as part of the village wall; its door was difficult to spot unless you knew it was there. Corvin had led Asha here for this reason. Outside, Asha could hear the cannibals whispering to each other. They sounded scared.

Corvin lay on his back and rested his head on Asha's thigh. Both his arm and leg were numb as his mind was wracked with memories. While Asha kept tapping him to make sure he didn't black out and slip into a coma, she did not take her eye away from the numerous glass spyholes that were mounted into the walls. They showed the village outside in wide, distorted angles, but they could not see her back. Hidden as they were, Asha knew they were trapped in this hut—only one way in and out. If they were spotted, they were dead.

They waited, but the cannibals did not leave. Soon it became dark. They did not light any torches, but soon the moonlight came pouring through the trees.

One of the cannibals cried out. Alarmed and anxious, Asha checked all of the spyholes until she saw what he was pointing at. The starless sky was clear. The moon was full again.

The scourge was coming.

THE FULL MOON SCOURGE

The cannibals fled the village in a hail of screams. The metal gate crashed as it flung open and they disappeared into the forest. Provided they could outrun the moonlight they would be safe. If not...

Asha waited until they had gone before frantically checking the entrance, making sure no light could enter the hut. She was rushing, she knew, but she forced herself to be precise. One small mistake now would mean death for them both. The rusted bolt on the door held tight and there were no gaps, holes, or crevices. The glass spyholes let no light in. The only thing illuminating the hut was a small plastic lantern that Corvin had wound up when they first entered. She looked at him now, lying on the floor, delirious, muttering to himself, while outside the full moon hung above the scrapyard. Its mercury light bathed the whole village. Through the spyholes, Asha saw wisps of white mist rising from the ground. Asha checked the hut over again.

Outside came the sounds of weeping. The scourge was here.

The whole village, the forest, the fields, the motorway, the entire country from coast to coast was alive with the cries of the dead. Voices so numerous it was impossible to distinguish one from the other as all those killed in The Return and all who had died since now walked, ethereal in the moonlight. Bringing nothing but memories, they mourned their existence and the hollow absence of life within them.

This was the full moon scourge. In the decades since The Return, people had learned only one safe recourse: hide. Right now, all over, families huddled together indoors and ran for cover, terrified for their lives. They plugged their children's ears and covered their own. Those stranded in the open took their own lives rather than suffering the fate of being touched by the ghosts of a world long dead.

After tearing strips from a sheet she found bundled in one corner and bandaging Corvin's wounds, Asha wound the lantern again and sat against wall, brought her knees up to her chin and covered her ears.

Corvin was pulled out of his delirium by a voice calling his name. It was deep, churned from inhaling too much smoke. When the voice let out a short, tickly cough, Corvin recognised it. He shot up, forgetting about his pains, and rushed to the spyholes. He saw the figure in the moonlight. And somehow, it saw him.

"Corvin!" The ghostly shape of the man cried, "Corvin, you have to help. It's horrible being dead, Corvin. There's nothing here. Just cold and black. It's awful. I'm cold, Corvin, please let me in." The scourge was at the door. Its ethereal hand reached for the handle, but passed right through.

"It's not really you, Richard. He's dead." Corvin shouted.

The deep voice outside turned to rage, "I know I'm dead, Corvin! You think I don't remember how you did it? Don't you remember? That's me over there, that pile of bones! The cuts still hurt, you know! They have done ever since! Don't try and make this any easier for yourself! I'm dead because of you! My kids are dead because of you!"

More voices joined as men and women, children of the village flocked to the hut. They called out to Corvin, begging to know why. When he didn't answer, their desperate cries became a cacophony of hatred.

"I was your friend!"

"I went easy on you whenever we fought!"

"It wasn't fair what we put you through, but you didn't have to do this!"

"Let me in, I just want to talk..."

"Did you do this to Sharon too?"

"Did we really deserve it, Corvin?"

"You were supposed to protect us!"

"You cold-blooded bastard, Corvin! I watched you murder them!"

"I hope you die slowly some day, just like I did!"

"I should have broken your neck in your sleep!"

"You're a failure, son. It was your job to see the Lesser one coming. But no, you were too busy with that girl. I thought I'd trained you better. I can't believe you're my son..."

The voices stopped as a cloud passed over the moon, blocking out the light. The scourge vanished and the village fell deathly silent. Asha, who had heard every word, clutched her cleaver tight against her chest. She glared at the man in black. The scourge hadn't given her a clear picture of happened, but she knew enough to be terrified of him.

The failed protector bowed his head. "I was meant to protect them," he whispered. The one-eyed woman's fear turned to pity.

Outside, the clouds completed their pass over the moon. Once again its light shone over the village. The scourge returned.

"Son," a lone voice spoke.

"No. You're dead." Corvin said.

"Son, I know I'm dead. I know. I'm sure you had your reasons, but son... I might have raised you hard—probably harder than anyone's ever been raised, but you're still alive because of it. How long's it been since you killed us? And how many fights have you won since? You're a protector. This village's first and last. We don't need your protection now, but you need ours. You're hurting, son. I can hear it in your voice. Just open the door and let me take a look at you. I need to see the man you've become. Please, I just need to see you're alright. Come on, son."

Corvin saw no reason not to. The bitter truth, the reason he wandered aimlessly for so long was because he no longer had a people to protect. His reasons to live had been taken from him. Killed by his own hand.

Let it take him then. Let it take the memories away. Let it make him not human. After all, what was the sense in wandering a dead world with nothing to search for? They were gone, she was gone, he couldn't even save Clara and Freya. Before long he'd be leaving Asha's corpse by the roadside too.

He reached for the door.

A hand grabbed his wrist. Gripping him tight, Asha pulled his arm back and shoved him against the wall, pinning her forearm across his throat. She held her cleaver high, ready to hack his arm off if he went to open the door again. As much as he longed for oblivion, he did not wish to spend his final moments as a maimed and bleeding thing. He relaxed, but Asha refused to lower the blade.

Outside, the scourge continued to curse Corvin.

SALTING THE MEAT

Asha woke with a start, brandishing her cleaver out to the darkness. She had not slept enough to forget where she was or what had happened—the words of the full moon scourge were still fresh in her mind. The lantern beside her had run out, so she wound it up and shone it around the small hut.

Corvin was gone.

Asha quickly gathered her things and headed out. It was almost mid-day, the black-scarred sun hung almost at its peak. The lingering dew made the air cold and the village somehow seemed more foreboding now than it had last night.

It took Asha longer than normal to locate Corvin's trail amidst all the cannibals', but eventually Asha found them. They led her all around the village, inside some of the metal huts, not moving in further than the threshold, then back like Corvin had been visiting these places. Eventually they led up to the iron gates and into the forest.

Corvin leaned against the crutch he'd made from a broken spear as he knelt down, wincing at the pain in his leg. The cave was small and dark—he had to hunch just to fit through the entrance—just enough room for him and the grave. As he brushed his fingers over the mound of smooth grey stones, he bowed his head.

No, it isn't a grave, he reminded himself. There's just dirt under those rocks. The body that should have laid there was destroyed. A part of him wanted to speak, tell her that he had avenged her like he promised, but another part of him asked what was the point? She was dead. She could not hear him. He was secretly relieved when she had not appeared with the scourge.

He sighed. His heart turned to granite. He was done with Asha's job. There was no reason in continuing with her. There was nothing in it for him. Enough was enough. He still didn't understand why he'd agreed to go with her so readily in the first place. She could easily pick up someone else along the way, but, he figured, she would do better to drop it altogether.

With the slightest of nods to the pile of stones, he pushed himself to his feet. He ducked underneath the cave entrance then staggered off into the forest. Where he was going, he didn't much care—the madness would only get worse, so one direction was as good as another.

When the pain in his leg became too severe he stopped at the next clearing and rested on a fallen tree trunk. Checking his bandages, the blood underneath had clotted and netted the material into his wounds. That the bleeding had stopped was a good sign, but that didn't mean he was safe. Aside from now being handicapped, he had infection to worry about too. After all, he'd seen smaller wounds bring down people bigger. He had no choice but to wait and deal with whatever happened.

He was not rested enough to carry on, but he wanted to get far away from this place as fast as possible. The wound in his leg sent pains all the way up one side as he stood up and started walking.

"Corvin?"

"Leave me alone, Asha." He muttered.

"Who's Asha? It's me, Corvin."

He stopped dead, "What? It's impossible..." He turned around.

She stood at the edge of the clearing, her white clothes were soiled with dirt, but her face and her bare arms were as clean and pale as they always were.

"Sharon..."

"You've finally come back." She smiled.

"I—" he could not find the words.

"Corvin, I missed you. Where did you go?" She walked towards him.

"I had to leave. After what I did..."

"But now they're all gone. There's no one to stop us being together now."

"Attachment is a threat. Safety is solitude." Corvin recited the mantra that had been burned into his memory.

"Those were your father's rules. He's not here to enforce them anymore." She held her arms out. Her soft skin yearned for his. "The dead can't judge us, Corvin."

It was not real. She wasn't really there. He was aware of this. In his mind a switch went off, informing him that the madness was now complete. This would be his end. But the flicker of warmth that ignited in his heart as she mouthed the last three words she had said to him before she died forced that knowledge to the back of his mind. Forgetting his wounds, Corvin took a step towards her and fell to one knee.

"Poor baby. Let me come to you. Let me protect you for once."

When she was just outside of reach, her head jerked back. Her long brown hair flung over her shoulders as the soft skin of her face split open. Bones broke, blood lashed into the air and floated weight-lessly.

Corvin looked on, paralyzed with horror. It was happening again. The same as last time.

But unlike last time, Sharon's body was not torn to shreds as the creature that wore her writhed free. Instead, she began to change. Her thin clothes fell, revealing a naked body that was not hers. This was shorter, thinner, with bruises covering the tops of her thighs. Her hands crossed in front of her face and once passed, Corvin saw a new face, pale, freckled, with crystal blue eyes, the very visage of innocence and fragility. The man in black knew this face also. But he also knew it was a disguise. He had seen the true form of the abomination beneath, the formless mass of tentacles and bones, of eyes and beaks, writhing, plotting, killing. This was the Lesser one that had bored into Sharon's flesh. This was the beast that had forced his hand. He thought he had destroyed it for good, but here it was.

It had returned.

Suddenly its true form burst from the girl's skin. It engulfed the man in black, pinning him to the ground as it constricted his whole body. The Lesser one writhed, emitting sounds that turned the blood cold. Suckers that covered its mass opened and closed in anticipation. Would it crush him? Break him? Devour him? He doubted it would let him die so quickly.

Then something happened that he did not expect. From its centre maw, the largest in the mass, a long black tongue flicked out and licked the cold sweat from his neck to his ear. It reared back, letting out satisfied groan, then licked the other side, engorging itself on his fear-born sweat.

This is wrong, Corvin realised, this Lesser one did not feed off flesh. Some may—they are different, indefinable—but this one sought to poison the mind and feed off the suppurations.

This thing was drinking his sweat. Eating his fear.

"Elsie!" A voice called.

Corvin barely heard it under the Lesser one's mass. The creature turned and suddenly its form changed again. Its appendages shrunk in and it became a fat man with a long, curved knife in one hand and a bloody wet eyeball in the other.

Asha froze.

"Your father won't be home until morning, little Asha," the man slurred. He took a drunken step towards her, almost tripping over Corvin.

Asha closed her lone eye. Beneath the scar tissue over her other socket, she felt phantom pains.

The fat man stroked his groin, "come here. You come here now. This is going to happen, little Asha, but if I have to come over there, I'll take your other eye out."

Corvin stood up and drew his fence blade. He had no doubts now that they had found the fear eater. With renewed vigour, he inched his way towards it. The fat man was getting angry that Asha was not doing as she was told.

When Corvin was within distance, he raised the fence blade, aiming to decapitate the fear eater in one swift blow.

"Corvin, don't!" Asha screamed.

The creature turned as Corvin swung.

Its disguises disappeared as a severed piece of it fell to the ground. They both saw the fear eater for what it was: an chitinous black creature, gaunt and hunched by its skeletal shape and unnaturally long legs. Were it able to stand upright it would have topped eight feet, but its narrow waist did not support the structure for it. Hundreds of needle-like teeth jutted from its narrow jaw and its eyes—the colour of bile— flared at the man in black.

The protector's face was a mask of pure hatred. This thing had re-enacted the worst moment of his life. It must be destroyed. The fence blade flashed in his hand. The fear eater nursed its arm where its hand had been severed. Green blood dripped. Before he could strike, the hunched monstrosity darted through the forest. Corvin could not give chase. Asha stood frozen. The fear eater was gone.

"What's the matter with you? We might never get an opportunity to kill it so easily again!" Corvin yelled at Asha. She didn't say anything. She stared at the forest where the fear eater had fled.

Corvin limped over to her, purposefully appearing to struggle. When he was close, he lunged. In one fluid motion, too quick for her to react, he had her off her feet and pushed her to the ground. She reached for the blade strapped to her belly, but Corvin got there first and disarmed her. He forced his weight down on top of her and pressed the edge of the blade to her throat.

"It's someone you know, isn't it? Elsie?" He said through gritted teeth.

She struggled. The blade edged closer to her neck.

"There is no contract, is there? You're hunting it for yourself. Who is it, mother? Sister? Friend? Tell me, or you die right here, Asha. And Elsie will be a monster until she dies of old age. You know it will kill anyone it comes into contact with. You should have killed Elsie as soon as the scourge touched her."

"I tried," Asha said.

"Well then you failed," he pushed the blade closer. A thin line of red appeared on her throat. "You're as bad as that old man back at the bar." In that moment, Corvin gasped as the realisation struck: the fear eater hadn't just appeared now, but had been with them since the beginning. The apparitions he'd been seeing of Freya and Clara, they weren't madness. "She hasn't been following me... She's been following you!"

"She's always following me," Asha choked, "I can always see her. Every minute of ev-every day, she's there. She stalks me."

"When did it happen?"

"Last winter."

"So everything you told me is a lie! Why are you only just hiring someone to hunt her down now?"

"I can ch-change her back. She can be my sister again."

"Impossible."

PROMISE OF REDEMPTION

It was a small metal box, small enough to sit in the palm of her hand. It had a flat bottom and a cog on the top that, when the handle at the side was turned, cranked a notched spool. Those notches struck tiny metal bars and made a sound. When Asha turned the handle quickly, the box played a sweet melody that Corvin recognised as something the elders used to hum to children.

"The seer said that if I can get her to hear this, it can force the scourge out of her and she'll be my Elsie again."

"How?" Corvin eyed the mechanism curiously. He reached for the music box, but Asha snatched her hand back.

"I don't know. I don't understand it. But he was certain it would work."

"Why did he give it to you?"

"He didn't. I bought it."

"With what?"

Asha slipped the box back in her pocket. "She ran that way. I don't know where she'll go though. I don't even know where we are, never mind what's over that way."

"It leads back to the motorway and a city at the very end."

"Which one?"

"They called it Manchester."

Asha looked at the ground and nodded. "You ever been there?"

"Only once." Corvin said darkly.

"We've got her trail," she started towards the patches of dank green blood on the ground.

"Wait. There's things we need first. Weapons."

"We're not killing her," she frowned.

"But we'll still need to defend ourselves in case we come across anything else. We should be quick though, before the blood dries and we lose the trail."

Asha helped Corvin back to the scrap village. He directed her to the largest settlement where a loose floorboard revealed a secret room underground. Winding another lantern, he showed Asha his father's weapon stash. He handed her a Taurus .38 Special revolver from the first workbench and took another one for himself. It looked tiny in his hand, but was heavier than it looked. The shiny nickel plating had worn off over the decades and the gun was coated in a thick layer of dust. He knew it might not work, but it was the risk you ran with anything from before The Return.

Asha tucked hers into her waistband at her back and Corvin hung his from a leather shoulder strap that he took down from the wall. They each grabbed as many cartridges as their pockets could hold. There were none for his Glock.

Most of the blades were too rusty to be of any use, but Corvin took a wooden mallet and instructed Asha to help herself while he headed to the far end of the room. He'd come for something specific.

Lying on its own table, Corvin pulled back the dusty white sheet and smirked when he saw only the slightest bit of rust on its blades and no rot on the shaft. The two blades were fierce—sharp on one edge and serrated on the other, they were slotted, glued and tied on to either side of the hard wooden shaft in between them. From tip to tip the weapon stood the same height as Corvin. Running his finger along both edges, he saw they were still sharp.

"My father made this for me. I'd just been appointed as protector and I was heading out to hunt a skin dweller. I was practically still a boy then."

"How long ago was that?"

"Eight winters, I think. I'm not sure. They blur

together." He lifted the twinblade from its wooden cradle. Balanced at either side, heavy, but not enough to make it unwieldy. He turned it over and the edge of the blades glinted in the lamplight. "There's one more thing."

They left the cellar and Corvin covered up the entrance with the loose floorboards. Asha followed him to an opened up building filled with tools and scrap metal. The man in black knelt down by a skeleton that was half-buried in the mud. "I need this, father," he whispered as he slid a metal brace off the femur and calf and strapped it around his own wounded leg. It felt strange having the brace on, but he felt the difference immediately. While he still limped, he could stand without aid.

"Let's go, before the trail goes cold."

GRAVES OF THE OLD WORLD

The sickly green blood stood out against the dirt. The distance between the splashes told them the fear eater was moving fast and hadn't slowed at all for miles. Corvin secretly hoped they would find the creature dead, having bled out from its wound, but for every mile they travelled, that hope faded a little more. If it was going to bleed to death, it would have done so by now.

Asha remained silent and pensive for the whole journey. More than once Corvin caught her staring at his twinblade, a look of concern on her face.

They took rest only when the pain in Corvin's leg became too intense. Though they were both hungry and exhausted—with Corvin's satchel abandoned they had lost their food—they did not have time to hunt or scavenge for more. Both of them secretly sensed the journey's end approaching; they rushed to meet it.

The blood led them through the ruins of another village and across miles of fields. The dirt paths eventually gave way to tarmac roads and concrete pavements as the towers of Manchester came into view. Huge structures of glass and metal and concrete loomed over the dead city. One was missing its entire side but was inexorably still standing, looking like it could collapse at any moment.

"Asha, do you know this place?"

She said nothing.

"Asha, tell me now." Corvin's hand went to his gun.

She nodded.

"So where is it going?"

"She."

Corvin frowned. Whoever it may have been before, it was now just a monster and no amount of correcting his terminology would change that. But he needed information she had. "Where is *she* going?"

"There's only one place I can think of."

"Which is?"

"To where the scourge touched her."

"What were you doing in the middle of a city? That's suicide."

"Hiding."

Corvin relaxed his hand, "well, since you know where she's going, you can go first."

The wind and its voices silenced as they entered the city. Sounds became muted like they were underwater. The thickness of it accentuated each noise they made and they became acutely aware of every footstep, every breath and even every heartbeat. Corvin did not know what caused this, but had been in enough cities to know it happened in all of them. People avoided them for this very reason. As soon as it came on, he remembered a theory he'd heard that the silence was the empty screams of those who died during The Return still echoing, untraceable by living ears.

However one sound cut clear through the murk. Corvin and Asha both startled as a shriek echoed a few streets away. Perhaps Elsie, now a product of The Return, could hear those silent screams?

They followed the scream into the city centre.

The buildings got taller and the silence became heavier, like a pressure building up inside their ears. Dust still polluted the air from when the buildings had collapsed. The few structures that were left intact were plastered with human remains, melted down and blasted onto the brickwork. No one knew exactly what happened when the Old Ones passed by the Earth, or why, but looking around, Corvin had an idea.

He kept his eyes firmly on where he was going.

"She'll be in the train station," Asha pointed up the slope to an enormous building. "That's where it happened."

The station was long, but not tall. The sloped pavement curved up and around and ended at a set of glass doors. Broken fragments still littered the ground. Asha entered first, then Corvin drew his Taurus and stepped over the threshold.

The inside of Piccadilly Station was huge and open-spaced. Almost pitch black save for the light filtering in where the ceiling had collapsed. The place smelled of damp. The ground was littered with debris and dripping water echoed from somewhere. Fragments of glass and bone crunched underfoot as Corvin stepped into the centre of the plaza, sticking close to the light. Beyond, he could make out rows of trains, now rusted to the spot.

He could hear breathing. As he peered into the dark corners he thumbed back the hammer on the .38 and readied his blade.

"Close your eyes, Asha. Or she'll appear as that man again."

"No. We need her alive."

Corvin swore under his breath. He wanted to tell her they must kill the creature while it was weakened, but he knew she wouldn't listen. She was blinded by love. He knew how that ended.

"Elsie!" Asha shouted, "Elsie, it's your sister!"

The breathing stopped. Then, all around them came a metallic chittering, followed by the grinding of teeth, a crying baby, a wheezing cough, a blaring horn, grunting, flesh beating against flesh, the mewing of a wounded animal, sobs, then a young girl whimpering, "Asha, please don't let him get me."

Corvin looked at Asha. She was in tears. He shook his head.

Then something pinned Corvin to the ground.

SAVIOUR

Corvin's gun went off as it flew from his hand. His twinblade skidded along the ground just out of reach. The fear eater's claws raked his back.

He swung his wounded arm around and struck the creature in its jaw. Fire erupted in his arm, but it bought him enough time to crawl forward and grab the haft of his twinblade. Rolling onto his back, Corvin swung his weapon, but hit nothing. The creature had disappeared. Corvin stood back up. Asha was sat on the ground, staring into space.

"You brought me here for this, woman! Are you going to let it kill us both? Because once it's done me, you'll be easy! You'll just let it happen!"

If she'd heard him, it didn't show.

He grabbed her. "It's not your sister anymore, Asha! It's a thing! An abomination!"

She pricked up at hearing her sister's name.

"You help me kill it, or it will kill us both!"

"No!" Asha screamed.

Corvin felt the barrel of her revolver press against his chin. He let go.

"It's watching us, you know. Can't you feel it?" he asked.

"Stop calling her 'it'," she stepped out of Corvin's reach.

"Is this why you hired me? Bait? Feed me to that monster while you put your trust in that little noise box?"

She grimaced. Her finger teased the trigger.

"There's no going back, Asha."

The hammer pulled back.

"Elsie is dead. She died here that night last winter."

Asha's gun fired.

The flash was blinding. The blast echoed all around

the train station, rattling the metalwork.

Corvin winced, then checked himself over. The shot had gone wide.

He looked at her. Her lone eye was wide, staring at something behind him.

He gripped the twinblade with both hands and swung it over his head, striking bony flesh. Corvin faced the creature, again it had taken the form of the lesser one, and attacked with his blades. Blood poured. Tentacles were severed and eyes were cleaved, but the creature refused to fall.

When the creature appeared to be stunned, Corvin glanced over his shoulder and saw Asha fumbling with her pockets. He turned back to the fear eater and stared into the soft eyes of Sharon.

"Corvin, don't do this. Please, you're hurting me." She held her bloodied hands up.

The words stabbed Corvin's heart, but he refused to let it hurt. He dropped the twinblade and wrapped his arms around Sharon, wrestling her to the ground and pinning her arms behind her back. The creature screamed in a perversion of Sharon's voice as Corvin used his weight to keep the fear eater down. "Now, Asha! The box!"

It was already in her hand. She turned the handle and the tiny cogs moved, ringing out a lullaby that echoed through the dead hall.

Monstrous sounds belched from Sharon's mouth. The skin of her cheeks shredded as her mouth jutted outwards, showing rows of needle-like teeth.

Asha kept turning the device. The music repeated. She moved closer.

The fear eater thrashed. Its guise disappeared and Corvin now straddled its true form. Bony, black, and stinking of rot.

Asha knelt by its head, still turning the music box. She stared imploringly into its cloudy yellow eyes. For a moment their eyes met and in them, Asha saw nothing but hunger.

Still she turned the handle.

Corvin could not hold the creature much longer. The wounds on his arm and leg screamed at him and the creature did not seem to be weakening. He made sure his twinblade was within reach for when it broke free.

Asha cried as she whispered softly to her sister.

Then Corvin was thrown clear. In a burst of strength, the fear eater rose up, slashed at Asha and ran for the man in black.

He was up and ready, the fence blade in one hand and the mallet in the other. He waited until it was close. Its claws, one mutilated, slashed at him wildly. Raw anger burned in its eyes as Corvin avoided its attacks. The more it missed, the more enraged it became. Corvin moved fast, skilfully, taking small counterstrikes where he could, not aiming to kill the creature, but incapacitate it. He broke its forearm with the mallet, slashed at its legs with the fence blade, hoping to sever a tendon.

It screeched as it lunged at him, aiming to shove its black claw through his face. The man in black bluffed to the side and brought the mallet down on its shoulder blade. There was a loud crack as its arm dislocated. In fury, the fear eater swung its loose arm, catching the protector unexpectedly and knocking him to the ground.

It stood over him now, snapping its bones back into place.

From its elongated maw it spoke in Sharon's voice, "I'm going to kill you now, my love. Like you killed me."

It lunged.

OBLIVION

As the rows of needle teeth punctured his neck, Corvin felt his body stiffen.

But then the teeth retracted. A sigh of stinking breath engulfed him and the beast fell. Corvin rolled away and stood up, checking his neck. He was bleeding, but it was not bad.

The fear eater lay on its back in a growing pool of its own blood. A hole struck in its chest had almost cleaved it in two. One end of his twinblade dripped with green blood—the smell was unbearable. Asha held it tight in her hands.

She stared down at the beast, but did not see the monster. Elsie lay on the ground in front of her. Just a young girl, less than half the age of her sister, she was still a child. Red blood dribbled from her mouth. She reached up, weakly, but her strength failed. As her skin grew paler, she mouthed words to Asha that never came. Then she convulsed and was still.

Asha fell to her knees and screamed. All the anger, guilt and despair she had carried rushed out of her in that cry and it echoed around the train station, lingering in the air long after the sound had abated. Corvin felt the intensity of it shudder through him. He stood there, unsettled. Helpless.

He stared at the body in front of them, wondering if the music box had worked, or if it had simply assumed the form of Asha's worst fear?

It was sunset when Asha finally got up to leave.

She said nothing for the rest of the night. She simply sat there, shoulders slouched, staring into the bonfire that Corvin had lit. The music box she had put so much faith in sat in the flames, its metal underside reddening in the heat. There were no tears, nor any hint of emotion or thought that crossed her face. Her lone eye was blank.

Corvin watched her from opposite the fire. He offered no words of comfort. He just sat, wrapped in his torn cloak. Beneath it, his hand rested on his gun.

He watched her very carefully.

When the fire began to burn out Corvin did not add anymore kindling. Still Asha did not move. Only when it was dark did he hear her lay down. Then Corvin did the same.

It was still night when he woke. The waning gibbous moon that shone down on Manchester seemed dimmer than usual. But it was not that which had woken him.

Someone was on top of him.

He heard breathing.

How had she managed to sneak so close? All of his training, the pains it took to sharpen his senses and she had bypassed it all. How?

He felt her breath on his neck. Her lips against his skin. The warm wetness of tears.

Her hands raked at his clothes in the dark, over the metal shoulder plates, down his chest and began unbuttoning his shirt. He opened his mouth to speak, but she kissed him.

He ran his hand down her side to where she kept the blade taped to her stomach. She tore it off, feeling her stiffen at the pain, and tossed it away. His shirt was now wide open. Her nails traced along his scars.

Corvin kissed her back, roving his hands over her flesh. Her leather jacket was already off. She gasped as he squeezed.

As the moon disappeared behind clouds, they felt their way around each other in the dark, probing, exploring, caressing the marks of each other's wounds. When Asha forced Corvin to enter her, he gasped. He had forgotten what it was like. He remembered quickly. Tears fell upon his bare chest.

It was not love. It was not repressed feelings. Corvin's flesh was just a bandage. She utilised him in order to feel something. In the warmth of his skin and the roughness of his touch, she found a moment of sanctuary, a brief respite that allowed her to forget, to be lost in something other than her own oblivion.

When it was over they fell asleep beside each other, cradled in each other's arms. She cried. And though she did not see it, Corvin shed a lone tear. One for every woman he had loved.

Corvin woke to a pale red sky. Cloudless. No wind. No sound. He sat up and winced as his pains awoke too. He looked at the desolate city around him. He could almost feel the silent screams in the cold tang of morning air.

He was alone.

He looked down at the patch of road beside him where Asha had laid. He put his hands to his chest where her tears had fallen. His skin was red, raised with scratch marks.

Asha was gone. Her clothes and belongings were missing too. Somehow she had dressed and taken them away in the night without making a sound. Corvin felt her absence in a way he had not expected.

He quickly dressed and gathered his things, hoping to pick up Asha's trail and catch up to her. After an hour of fruitless searching, growing more and more hopeless, he found the faintest hint. Corvin's heart leapt as hope returned and he raced onwards.

But the trail split soon into three separate routes. Asha had covered her tracks well, he realised. She must have known he would try to follow her and had left dummy trails to stop him.

Only those who wished not to be found did this.

Hope left him and his heart weighed heavy. It was

only then that Corvin understood why he had followed her so readily in the first place.

He turned away from the trails and headed back through Manchester. Another tear stained his cheek as he walked through the city and into the wilderness beyond.

Alone.

Shades of Oblivion

CPSIA information can be obtained
at www.ICGtesting.com
Printed in the USA
BVHW041656270220
573548BV00004B/14/J